A Highlander's Vow

The Mackenzies of Castle Leod
Book 2

Callie Hutton

ARE YOU SIGNED UP FOR DRAGONBLADE'S BLOG?

You'll get the latest news and information on exclusive giveaways, exclusive excerpts, coming releases, sales, free books, cover reveals and more.

Check out our complete list of authors, too!

No spam, no junk. That's a promise!

Sign Up Here

www.dragonbladepublishing.com

Dearest Reader;

Thank you for your support of a small press. At Dragonblade Publishing, we strive to bring you the highest quality Historical Romance from some of the best authors in the business. Without your support, there is no 'us', so we sincerely hope you adore these stories and find some new favorite authors along the way.

Happy Reading!

CEO, Dragonblade Publishing

Additional Dragonblade books by Author Callie Hutton

The Mackenzies of Castle Leod
A Highlander's Bride (Book 1)
A Highlander's Vow (Book 2)
A Highlander's Heart (Book 3)

The Lyon's Den Series
The Lyon and the Lass

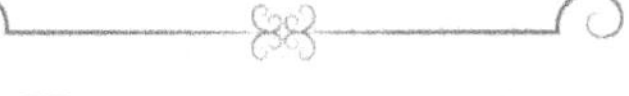

PROLOGUE

Castle Leod
Scottish Highlands
Late Fall 1729

GREGORY MACKENZIE JOINED his cousin, Laird Daniel Mackenzie, and his wife Beth at the table in the Great Hall at Castle Leod, more than ready for his supper. As second-in-command to the laird, Gregory had just spent hours on the lists, training new warriors who had a lot more swagger than they did common sense and ability.

Was he ever that young?

He settled into the seat next to Daniel, who was busy filling his plate. "How did the training go?" the laird asked.

Gregory grinned and began to fill his own plate. "The lads in this new group are going to have to be smacked down a few times before they get some idea of what a warrior is. Right now they're busy strutting in front of the lasses."

Daniel chuckled. "Mayhap you, me, and a few of the others should take them on. Have them groaning with aches and pains. 'Tis hard to chase the ladies when ye smell like the healer's cream."

Beth looked over to the two men, a smirk on her face. "And I assume neither one of ye had an overblown image of yerselves when ye were lads."

Daniel leaned toward her, a smile on his lips. "Now, love, I was always a serious warrior-in-training."

Gregory laughed. "Shall I tell yer charming wife about the time that ye and Francis—"

"There is no need to spread tales, cousin," Daniel said, then looked up as one of his men approached the table. "Yes, John?"

"This message just came for Gregory."

Gregory put his hand out and took the paper.

'Twas not often that he received messages, so with a bit of curiosity he opened the parchment and read the words. He felt the blood rush from his face. Shaking his head he read the document over again. His mouth dry, he looked up at his cousin. "I canno' believe it."

"What is it?" Daniel asked, frowning. Beth leaned forward so she could see past her husband to Gregory.

Gregory ran his fingers through his hair. "I ken ye heard me speak of Robert Sinclair? We trained together at Dornoch Castle years ago."

Daniel nodded. "Aye. I remember ye speaking of him and also him stopping here a couple times for a visit while on his various travels for his da."

Gregory took a deep breath and shook his head again as if clearing his brain. "He was killed in a minor skirmish on one of the Sinclair borders."

Beth's hand flew to her mouth. "Oh, my. How terrible."

"Aye," Gregory said. He folded the parchment and turned to Daniel. "I will need to go to Castle Sinclair Girnigoe."

Daniel frowned. "'Twill be much too late for the funeral. 'Tis a four, or maybe five day trip up there."

Gregory sighed and stared into space for a minute. "I ken that, but there is another reason I must pack up and go immediately."

Daniel and Beth looked at each other and then back at Gregory, curiosity on their faces. "Aye?" Daniel asked.

Gregory stared at the note in his shaky hand. "Years ago, after seeing one of the best warriors struck down in another minor skirmish, leaving behind a wife and a few bairns, we made a vow to each other that if one of us died, the other would marry his widow, if he was no' already married." He shook his head and smiled. "We even wrote it down." He waved the old-looking piece of paper. "This is the pledge, and someone from his clan sent it, along with a short note that Robert had died."

He looked at his cousin and sucked in a deep breath. "I need to travel to Sinclair Castle Girnigoe and fetch my wife."

CHAPTER ONE

Later that evening

AFTER PREPARING FOR his departure the next morning, Gregory joined Daniel in his solar. Beth had retired for the evening and it was just the two of them sipping ale and watching the small fire burn down.

At last, Daniel, most likely thinking of his wife all soft and warm waiting for him in their bedchamber, broke the stillness. "You've never been one to shirk a vow, Gregory. So why does this one trouble you so? I get the impression that you seem to think marrying Megan Sinclair is akin to a noose about your neck."

Gregory gave a humorless laugh. "Because it is. Marriage was never meant for me."

Daniel arched a brow. "You've said as much before. But you've never told me why."

For a long while Gregory continued to stare into the fire. Then, as though the words dragged themselves out of him, he spoke. "When I was but a lad, I watched my mother's eyes grow sad with disappointment and misery over the years of her marriage.

"My father was a hard man. He cared more for alliances and land than for her. She was given to him by her da like coin traded across a table, and he demanded from her obedience, sons, and silence. No'hing else.

"He also had no problem taking his fists to her. After a beating, I would hide under my bed and listen to her crying."

Daniel's jaw tightened, but Gregory continued.

"I swore I'd never bind a woman to me that way. Never make her feel as though she meant less to me than the sheep in the pasture. And I would ne'er take my fists to her."

Daniel's eyebrows rose. "Nay. Ye are no' a mon to harm someone under yer care."

He looked at Daniel. "And then…" His voice roughened. "Then I tried once. There was a lass, years ago, before I came here from Fairburn Tower to act as your Second-in-Command. I thought… perhaps."

He shrugged and took a gulp of his ale. "She died before winter ended. Fever took her so swiftly, I scarce had time to understand what I felt for her before she was gone."

Gregory smiled. "I believed it was fate's way of reminding me that marriage for me is no' meant to be."

The solar fell quiet but for the crackle of flame. Two men sitting there with their own thoughts. Daniel with his happy marriage that took him forever to talk his wife into.

Gregory rubbed a hand over his face, weariness making him appear much older than his twenty-eight years. "Since then I've held to my oath. I'll fight for my clan, bleed for them, die for them if need be. But I'll not bind a woman to me and watch her suffer and fade." He shrugged. "Mayhap I have my da in me and will turn on any wife I take."

Daniel leaned forward, resting his arms on his thighs. "Ye've spent too much time alone, cousin. Ye are yer own mon, not a copy of yer da. Since it seems ye are headed to the state of marriage, consider it need not be a chain, nor something that will turn ye into a mon ye would ne'er be." He sat back in his seat. "The elders gave me two choices for a bride and I thank the Lord every day that I was able to convince my Beth to marry me. She has shown me what love really is. 'Tis a great thing, ye ken."

Gregory's mouth twisted. "Aye, well. Ye've always had more

faith in love than I."

He stood and nodded to Daniel. "I leave at first light. If I doona see ye before I leave, I will honor my vow and return with a wife."

Daniel nodded and watched his cousin leave.

As planned, Gregory and the half dozen men Daniel sent with him were mounted and on their way to Sinclair Castle Girnigoe before the sun rose.

The night before, while tossing and turning, punching his pillow every half hour or so, Gregory had plenty of time to think about his life and the changes he was about to face. *A wife.* Something he hadn't planned on. Certainly not for a long time.

He'd had plenty of lasses, but never one who expected more than a tumble in bed and in some cases, a coin or two. Sometimes he felt as though that whole process left him feeling empty, but a man had needs.

He spent a great deal of time wondering how he was going to approach Robert's widow. Did she know about the pledge they had made? Were there several bairns to bring back with him? Would the woman even honor the agreement made so long ago?

Gregory had never met Robert's wife. The two men weren't the best in keeping up correspondence. Robert had stopped a few times at Castle Leod before he married Megan.

It had been a joy to reunite with his friend. They wrestled, clashed over swords, drank the village inn dry, and had fun with a couple of lasses. At the same time.

Robert had never mentioned plans to take a wife, so getting the message telling him of Robert's death and enclosing the document with the pledge they'd made to each other when they were barely twenty years had been a shock.

Gregory had no idea who'd had possession of the document

to send it to him. It would have been better if the sender had enclosed more information than *"Robert is dead from a skirmish on the border. He asked me years ago to hold this and send it to you if he should die, leaving a wife."*

And there in his hand was the note from so long ago, with the words of the pledge and his signature, along with Robert's scrawl.

There was no mention of bairns, so Gregory was left to wonder if he was bringing back an entire family or one woman.

LADY MEGAN SINCLAIR sat on her bed and studied the tree that grew outside, right in front of her window. Again, she wondered if she should crawl over the opening and climb down the tree to escape.

The first clumps of dirt had just hit her husband's body when his uncle, the new Laird Anthony Sinclair, told her without any care that he was arranging a marriage for her.

When shock and anger had overtaken her, she'd lashed out at the man. For her trouble, she had ended up in her locked bedchamber with no more information on Uncle Anthony's announcement. Since that day, she'd been ordered to remain there with meals sent up to her.

She didn't want another husband. Robert had not been a mean man, but she had never felt a connection between them. *Aloof, indifferent, cold.* Any one of those words would have fit her husband and their marriage.

She and Robert had been married to fulfill a betrothal between Megan's da, Laird Monro, and The Sinclair, Robert's father. She'd reluctantly accepted it. Although 'twas not an uncommon practice, she had hoped to skip her obligation to her clan and choose her own husband, someone who would love her and accept her love for him.

No more than a few months after their marriage, the laird died from the heart issues he'd been suffering with for years.

Robert was then immediately thrust into the position of Laird Sinclair. He had not been properly prepared for the role and she oftentimes thought that was when he had begun to withdraw from her.

Although her husband had known all his life that he was the next laird when his da passed, he had not been given enough training for the position. Robert had seemed to use his title as laird to impress the clan members and, she was certain, to attract a number of lasses to bed. He strutted around, seeming to forget he had duties to go with the title.

Robert's Uncle Anthony took over the role of laird, claiming to offer advice to Robert to such an extent that her husband eventually stepped back and let his uncle take over.

Freed from the responsibilities, Robert continued to spend his time visiting the local ale house, training on the lists, and taking a tumble with one or more of their maids.

A few times Robert made the effort to take back his duties, but power-hungry Uncle Anthony was not willing to step back.

In the almost two years of their marriage, no bairns appeared, which became another point of contention between them. Despite Robert's claims to the contrary, if she was indeed barren as the healer had suggested to her, it was not something she planned, or did on purpose.

She sighed, going over those things in her mind when she was interrupted by a knock on her bedchamber door. It was not time for supper yet, so she was surprised to be disturbed.

The locked turned and the door opened. One of the young chambermaids stood there. "The new laird wishes to see ye in his solar."

The new laird.

She shook her head. No, with Robert not willing to do his duty, Anthony had been laird since Robert's da had died.

Megan wiped her damp palms on her dress and followed the maid to the solar. She should have freshened up and brushed her hair, but with her lack of interest in Anthony, she didn't care.

The man sat at the desk in what should have been Robert's solar, that he had seldom visited.

"Ah, my dear niece." He waved to one of the chairs in the solar. "Please have a seat."

She raised her chin and looked him in the eyes. Remaining standing, she said, "What is it ye want with me?"

Anthony leaned back and studied her. "Ye are a pleasant-looking woman. Yer attitude could use some attention, but in any event, I have arranged a marriage for ye to Laird Stephen Gunn. Yer marriage to the laird would make for a strong alliance."

"The Gunn is a small clan, how would ye benefit?"

"It will strengthen us against the encroaching Sutherlands, who are causing issues on the border with us."

"Ye're no' as wise as ye think. The Sutherlands could wipe ye out without the help of any other clan. Uniting with the Gunns gives ye no advantage."

Anthony slammed his fist on the desk, his face twisted and red with anger. "Ye think ye ken so much. As a woman ye need to learn yer place." He stabbed himself in the chest with his thumb. "I am yer laird and I make the decisions."

Not one to submit to this man's demands, she narrowed her eyes. "What else are ye gaining?"

"'Tis none of yer business. Now prepare for yer marriage. We leave first thing in the morning."

"I think no'." Megan shook her head. The Gunn was old enough to be her grandfather. He was smelly, almost bald, and had sausage fingers that she couldn't imagine touching her. He'd already gone through two wives in the hopes of a son, and Megan wasn't convinced he didn't "help" them to meet their end when he grew tired of them.

Before Anthony could reach across the table and use his fist on her—which he had done before—she added, "'Tis too soon after Robert's death. The priest willna' allow it."

"I'll see that he allows it." He slammed his hand on the desk again, almost rattling her teeth. "He needs an heir."

Megan tilted her head and looked at the man. "Dinna' ye accuse me of being barren? Did ye share that information with The Gunn?"

A knock on the solar door had them both turning toward the maid standing there. "My Laird, there is a gentleman here asking for Lady Sinclair."

CHAPTER TWO

GREGORY HAD AN uncomfortable feeling about Clan Sinclair even before he and his men were told to wait in the great hall for Lady Sinclair. No offer was made for drink or food always given to a traveler.

He'd expected a different sort of Clan Sinclair. True, he hadn't spent much time with Robert over the years, but the Robert he'd known would never allow the sloppiness of the warriors training on the lists that they'd seen on their way in.

It was the middle of the day and men were slouching around the great hall drinking ale. Maids who appeared to be cleaning up the area from the noon meal seemed more interested in the men who kept waving ale glasses in the air for a refill.

Even as he watched, a lass sat grinning on a warrior's lap, his hand busy down her bodice. Gregory shook his head. What the hell had happened to his friend's clan?

At the sound of someone approaching him, he turned to spot a woman. Her body was the kind that gave a man visions of nights spent in bed with low candlelight and a bottle of wine. Her delicious curves filled out her bodice well, and her small waist brought attention to hips that a man could hold onto. Those curves, along with her full lips, made her very appealing.

She had a sprinkling of freckles over her creamy cheeks, green eyes, with long lashes, and golden-red hair held back from her face with two braids fastened at the back of her head. He hoped with all his heart that this was Robert's widow. For as much as he didn't want to marry, he would have no problem bedding this beauty.

She stopped in front of him, tilting her head in question. "Ye wish to see me?"

"Aye." All of a sudden, he found it hard to even speak with her deep green eyes boring a hole into him. His mouth had dried up and he knew he had a silly grin on his face.

"What is it ye want from me, sir?"

Ach lass, if I told ye what I wanted from ye, I would get a slap in the face, or a dirk in my neck.

Gregory cleared his throat. "Are ye Robert Sinclair's widow?"

She stared at him for a moment, then nodded. "Aye, I am Lady Megan Sinclair."

Still unable to form words, he fumbled in the pocket of his trews and withdrew the note that had been penned by Robert and sent to Gregory from someone in the clan. Finding his voice, he said, "Yer husband and I drew this up when we were young warriors training together at Clan Sutherland."

Before she even looked at the words her husband had written, her eyes lit up. "Ye are Gregory Sinclair?"

He nodded.

Her face became very animated. "He spoke of ye often. He always wanted us to take a trip to Castle Leod for a visit."

Noticing the interest from others in the great hall, he took Lady Sinclair by her elbow and walked her away from questioning eyes. "Is there somewhere we can speak privately?"

If she was surprised by his words, she didn't show it. She nodded and said, "Upstairs is my sitting room. We can go there."

He nodded and motioned to his men to wait for him.

She chatted all the way up the stairs and down the corridor to her sitting room. She kept glancing over her shoulder at him, the words spilling from her mouth until he was concerned she would lose her balance and tumble down the stairs.

Once they were settled in the small room with two chairs, neither of which look as though they would hold him, he took a deep breath. "Please read the note I gave you."

She startled, almost as if she had forgotten the parchment in her hand. She opened it and her eyes moved back and forth over the words. Megan sucked in a deep breath. She placed her hand on her chest and looked at him with tears in her eyes. "What does this mean?"

He nodded at the paper. "Just what it says. As young warriors Robert and I saw a mon cut down in battle who left a young wife and two bairns. We decided then and there that we would ne'er allow that to happen to either one of us."

She licked her lips and whispered, "Meaning…what?"

He stood and ran his fingers through his hair. "Meaning, Lady Sinclair, I intend to fulfill our pledge."

When she continued to stare at him, he huffed, "I am here at Sinclair Castle Girnigoe to marry ye."

⤞⤜

MEGAN COULD ONLY stare at the man. He was here at Sinclair Castle Girnigoe to marry her?

To marry her?

She was in the middle of an argument with Anthony about not wanting to marry the old Gunn laird and this one showed up with a note that, he told her, said that as Robert's widow, she had to marry *him.*

At least he was young, handsome, and had all his teeth. But she didn't want another husband. At least not now. She would like some freedom. And she was tired of being told what she *had* to do and who she *had* to marry. Robert was a husband who she hadn't chosen either.

Now this man cleared his throat and stood before her, his giant hands on his hips. "Is there a problem, lass? Is there another mon ye are hoping to marry?"

She slowly shook her head. "Nay. I doona wish to marry anyone. My husband is in his grave less than one moon. I am trying to explain that to the laird, who wants to ship me off to another husband of his choosing right away."

Gregory nodded. "Aye, I agree with ye there lass. 'Tis too soon for another husband. But my pledge is to keep ye safe, so ye will return with me to Castle Leod and we can marry when yer feelings have settled."

She sucked in such a huge breath at his arrogance that she began to cough. He looked at her with alarm. She pointed to the table near her small desk where a cup of ale sat.

He brought it to her and she drank it down, her throat easing.

The man walked in circles. "I doona think I did this the right way."

"I hate to discourage ye further, but there is no right way." Her voice still sounded scratchy.

He nodded at the message in her hand. "Do ye recognize yer husband's handwriting?"

She shrugged. "I guess. I doona think I saw his handwriting more than a couple of times."

"Can I ask ye this, lass. Do ye want to marry this mon yer uncle has chosen for ye?"

She shook her head vigorously. "Nay! I doona want to marry any mon that someone picked for me." Her voice became a whisper, "Especially that one."

Gregory tried to hide his grin but was not successful, which appeared to anger her further. "Ye are like all men. Ye think women have no brains and can't make decisions for themselves. I ken who I want to marry and who I doona want to marry. I doona need another mon to tell me."

"Then who is it ye want to marry, lass? As long as I see ye settled with a good mon, I will feel as though I have fulfilled my obligation to Robert."

She stamped her foot. "That is what I mean. Ye will decide

who will suit for my husband." She poked herself in the chest. "That decision will be mine."

The door to the sitting room opened and a man entered. "Who is this mon who sent for ye? And why are ye meeting him in yer sitting room with no chaperone?"

Megan closed her eyes and sighed. "This is Gregory Mackenize. He has come to marry me." She stated it that way only to get a reaction from Anthony.

Which she did.

"Nay!" He waved his hand around. He turned toward Gregory, his hands fisted at his side. "What right do ye have to claim my niece?"

He nodded to the note in Megan's hand. "An agreement between myself and Robert Sinclair."

"Laird Robert Sinclair is dead. I am the new laird and all agreements must be approved by me." Anthony pointed his finger at the parchment Megan clutched. "How do I ken this is real? It could be something ye made up when ye heard about my nephew's death. What is in it for ye? Have ye always been sniffing around Megan's skirts?"

When Gregory made a move to go after Anthony, two of the laird's men pulled their swords and stepped forward, placing their swords on his chest.

Anthony waved them back. "Even if it is real, 'tis no' a formal betrothal. She is going to marry Laird Gunn."

Gregory looked between her and Anthony. "I doona think the lass agrees with that."

Anthony pounded his fist on a nearby table. "She has no choice. I made the agreement with The Gunn. We leave tomorrow first light to bring her to Clyth Castle where she will honor the betrothal I made." He pointed his finger at Gregory. "Ye will leave now."

Megan felt her first flash of panic. As much as she had no interest in marrying again, if she didn't go with Gregory, she would be swept away by her uncle and married to The Gunn before the sun set the next day.

She looked frantically at Gregory Mackenzie with hope. The lesser of two evils.

CHAPTER THREE

GREGORY READ THE panic in Lady Sinclair's eyes. He had no intention of leaving the lass here to be shuffled off to an old man. His honor was at stake as well as his care for the lass.

The six warriors who came with him were still down in the great hall. Trying to grab her now and making an escape was not a good idea. The lass could be hurt in the battle that would erupt.

"I'm no' going to fight ye," he said. When he heard Megan's sharp intake of breath, he turned and winked at her. Hoping she was a bright woman, and had already sensed his honor, she would understand this was not finished.

Gregory turned and left the room and headed downstairs. He waved at his men with him and they followed him out the door.

"What about the lass?"

"We will get her, but we have to make some plans." He led them to the stables and, making sure the grooms heard them, he talked to the men about the best way to return to Castle Leod.

They fetched their horses and rode off. After a few miles, Gregory held up his hand, and the men stopped. "What's going on, mon?" Francis, one of the men with them asked. "I thought we were bringing the lass back with us."

Gregory swung off his horse, Apex, and led him to a small creek. The men followed him and once the horses were watered and hobbled, they all sat in a circle.

"'Tis not going to be as easy as I would like."

Francis huffed and pulled a blade of grass and bit into it. "Most things are no' easy."

"There is an uncle there. The new Laird Sinclair. He has plans for the lass to marry the head of the Gunn clan. I ken the mon myself. He's old, never misses a meal, and I canno' imagine, nor allow, The Gunn to climb into bed with Megan Sinclair."

"Robert's widow?" John asked.

Gregory nodded.

"But ye can imagine yerself crawling into bed with the lass?" Callum, another warrior on the journey, said with a grin on his face.

Gregory smacked him in the back of his head and frowned. "We need a plan. The Sinclair is leaving at first light tomorrow to bring the lass to Clyth Castle. For as anxious as The Sinclair is to marry the lass off, I imagine they will perform the ceremony the minute they arrive."

"So we must get her out of there as quickly as possible," Alexander said.

"Aye. It's either that or try to take her on the road, to Clyth Castle where there would be a chance of her being hurt. After seeing Robert's uncle's determination, and how quickly after his nephew's demise this is all happening, there must be something big in it for him."

"Do ye think he had something to do with Robert's death?"

Gregory shrugged. "Unfortunately, we won't have time to dwell on that. After Lady Sinclair and I are married, I might look into it, but no' until the lass is safe from the uncle."

After Lady Sinclair and I are married.

It amazed him how smoothly and quickly that statement came out. He'd never thought to be a married man.

ONCE GREGORY LEFT the castle, Uncle Anthony ordered Megan to her bedchamber. He followed her and stood in the middle of the room with his hands on his hips, scowling. "I doona believe that message for one minute. The man is an outsider opportunist. And, how did he even get that piece of parchment?"

Megan hadn't given that thought any consideration. She had heard Robert speak of Gregory Mackenize, but since she'd never met him, this man could be an imposter who just made this up.

Now neither one of her choices seemed safe. Be hauled off to Clyth Castle and married to an old, smelly man, or rescued by a man she'd never met before, and had no reason to trust.

Even if he was the handsomest man she'd ever met.

In between bouts of anger, she'd been taken by his wavy, dark brown hair, deep blue eyes, and warrior's body.

Anthony turned toward the door. "Pack yer belongings, lass. Ye will remain here until morning when we leave. I will have one of the maids bring yer supper."

He and his two warriors left the room, slamming and locking the door.

Megan sat on her bed and hugged her stomach. There was no one to trust. Aye, Robert had mentioned Gregory a few times before and told her stories of their antics when they were training at Dornoch Castle. But was the message he brought with him real? Why hadn't Robert mentioned it to her?

She eyed the window in her bedchamber again. If she waited until her supper was brought, no one would enter her bedchamber again until they came for her the next morning.

She walked to the window and looked down. It was quite a drop, but she could do it. The question was, what would she do once she was on the ground?

'Twas possible she could steal a horse from the stable, but go where? Plus, the dangers on the road were worse than what she could face with either Gregory Mackenzie or The Gunn.

With a deep sigh, she laid on the bed and stared at the canopy over her head. 'Twas not like her to give up, but she had no idea how to avoid her fate.

She rolled to one side and remembered Gregory winking at her when he'd left. For a warrior, she'd thought he'd given up too easily. Was that a sort of signal from him that he would not leave her to the fate Anthony planned?

Many sleepless nights caught up with her and she was sound asleep when the click of her bedchamber door lock woke her up. A maid entered with a supper tray. She placed it on the table by her bed and left, re-locking the door without saying a word. Most likely under orders from Anthony.

She had to force herself to eat, but with no idea what her fate was, she needed her strength. If she decided to escape, it might very well be the last meal she ate for a while.

"How well-guarded do ye think the lass is?" Francis asked as the six warriors and Gregory sat around the small fire they'd made, eating the few rabbits and fish they'd caught earlier. It was growing past gloaming and they would soon have to make their move to rescue Megan.

"I'm sure she's locked in her bedchamber," Gregory said.

Malcolm looked over at Gregory. "They might have one of his men in her room."

Gregory shook his head. "First, he has no reason to believe she will try to escape with her door being locked. Then we made sure they think we're on our way back to Castle Leod.

"And it doesn't seem likely to have a mon in her room all night if they plan to pass her off to The Gunn tomorrow, looking as though she'd been raped," Gregory said as he stabbed another piece of meat.

"Aye, I doubt he would be happy to know that the woman he's marrying could be pregnant by another man," Peter added.

"Or, given his age and lack of an heir he might verra well be happy about it," Peter said with a grin.

They seven men remained silent, considering what Peter had just said.

"What is the plan, then?" John asked.

"The keep, or even the castle, doesn't seem well guarded and since about half the men in the great hall were busy fondling the maids and drinking in the middle of the day, I think by the time it's dark one of us could easily slip in and get the information from a very cooperative maid," Gregory said with a grin, "about where Lady Sinclair bedchamber is located and if her door is locked, or if a mon stands guard."

He stood and stretched. "But no' me," he added. "I'm sure anyone would remember me since I met with Lady Sinclair and the uncle in the great hall, while any one of you would not necessarily be noticed."

"What do ye plan to do with the information then, break into her room?" Alexander asked.

"That will be decided once we find out where the lass is and what sort of guard she has." He placed his hands on his hips and stared out at the beauty of the Highlands. "If we can't get her tonight, we'll have to grab her tomorrow on their way to Clyth Castle which I doona want to do."

"So who will go to the great hall and get the information?" Peter asked.

"I will," all six men quickly answered.

Gregory burst out laughing. "Ye forget whoever goes on the mission is not only there for some drink and tupping."

A few hours later, Francis, the most ordinary looking of the men, left for the castle.

The rest of them sat around the fire, Gregory mostly planning in his mind how they would get the lass out with the information Francis would hopefully return with. He did not want to try to snatch the lass back while they traveled. That was too risky.

"Ye ne'er mentioned marriage before, Gregory. Are ye sure ye want to do this?" John asked. "And what if his widow doesn't want ye?"

"I wouldn't blame her, and she's already said so," Gregory replied with a soft laugh. "I'm not the man most lasses dream of. I have no idea how to offer sweet words. But I can keep her safe. I can keep her free from men like the one her uncle's chosen."

A long pause followed as Gregory thought once again about how his life would change. Then, quieter he added: "But if she asks me to leave her be, I will. I'll protect her from other men even if I can't call her mine."

Chapter Four

Francis had lost his joy in drinking and fondling the maids who so easily offered themselves up to him. Gregory was counting on him, so he had to remind himself this was not a party, but a serious attempt to find out where Lady Sinclair was being held and how determined her guard was.

So far he'd learned that the lady of the manor was in her bedroom and he just now learned from another lass that the door was locked. This pretty little one waved the key to Lady Sinclair's room that she kept on a chain around her neck, in his face.

"Why would the laird trust ye with the key?" he asked as he slid his hand up the inside of her leg.

"Because he kens I will go to his bed anytime he asks." She giggled. "Some of the others avoid him because he can be a bit rough at times."

Francis frowned. "And that doesna bother ye?"

She shook her head, but there was a definite sense of pain in her eyes. "He gives me the easier jobs and time off that the others doona get."

He grinned to himself. It appeared he would have to make the sacrifice and entice the lass into one of the bedrooms in order to relieve her of the key. It would be necessary to make sure she had enough to drink so she wouldn't raise an alarm after he left.

He placed his hands on her face and pulled her close.

"What are ye doing?" She giggled again.

"Kissing the prettiest lass in the room."

She sighed. Obviously, the lass received very little in the way of praise from The Sinclair when she was warming his bed. She settled for the easiest jobs and extra time off.

While he was busy with her mouth, he waved at one of the lasses to bring them the whisky that she was handing out to the other warriors.

If this was a clan they wanted to conquer, all they had to do was attack at night. The few warriors he saw up on the ramparts when he easily slipped into the keep were too busy sipping ale and bragging to each other to pay much attention to what was going on outside the castle. 'Twas information to pass along to Gregory.

It took him no more than a half hour to douse the lass with whisky, have her take him to a bedroom, do what he needed to do—oh the sacrifice!—and leave with the key in his pouch. She was naked and snoring when he left. He'd pulled a cover over her body then looked at her for a minute. 'Twas a sad life for the lass to be sure. He was almost tempted to bring her with him, but they didn't need that complication.

He walked the distance to where he'd left his horse and headed back to the other warriors, whistling a tune. 'Twas too bad not all his assignments were such as this.

"It took ye long enough," Gregory groused when he returned and slid off his horse. "I still need to get the lass out and as far away as we can get in the dark."

Francis raised his eyebrows and dangled the key in front of Gregory. "'Twas no' an easy assignment. However, Lady Sinclair is in her bedchamber upstairs, with the door locked."

Gregory placed his fists on his hips. "And what good is the key to the lass's bedroom? Am I to stroll into the keep and make my way up the stairs and bring her down?"

Francis nodded. "That's about it. Ye wouldna' ken how sloppy the keep is. I doona think there was a sober head in the place.

Even the men up on the ramparts were chatting away like a couple of old women and drinking ale."

"What about The Sinclair?"

He shrugged. "I have no idea. I met one of the lasses who services him—she is the one I got the key from, and doona ask how—and she said he rarely appears downstairs after the evening meal."

"I canno' believe the mon I spent time with at Dornoch Castle would allow such a thing in his keep," Gregory said.

Francis shrugged. "The mon ye spent time with is dead, but I will say things couldn't have changed that much in the few weeks since he died.

"However, when questioned, the lass I got the key from mentioned that Robert Sinclair had stepped back and the uncle had been acting as laird since the old laird died."

Gregory shook his head. "All this chatting away is no' getting us Lady Sinclair and on the road." He gestured to Peter. "Go steal a horse from the Sinclair stable for Lady Sinclair. We might as well get this over with and on our way."

Gregory urged his horse forward and swung his leg over the animal's back. "Be ready to leave the minute I return with the lass. I want to get as far away from here as we can and with it being dark, it will be slow going."

'Twas a short ride to Sinclair Castle Girnigoe. He could hear the noise of the gaiety long before he approached the gate to the castle, which was wide open. There were no men on the ramparts. Chances were, from what Francis told him, the men were fast asleep by now. He shook his head, thinking that either the Sutherlands or the Mackays should take over the Sinclair land. Such a lax in guarding their castle actually made it dangerous for the clans surrounding it.

He walked into the great hall with his hand on his sword, not sure if things were as bad as Francis said.

They were.

He walked through the hall, up the stairs, and tried each door latch. The only one locked must have been Lady Sinclair's. He pulled the key from his pouch and fitted it into the hole, twisting it until it unlatched. Then he opened the door. Slowly at first.

'Twas dark in the room, but not dark enough to hide the woman crawling out the window onto the branch from a tree outside her window.

Gregory sucked in a breath, but didn't want to startle the lass by calling out to her. Instead, he quickly left the room, and raced down the stairs and through the keep, rounded the building and reached the tree just as Megan started to climb down.

"Doona move lass," he said quietly enough not to have her fall. However, it didn't work and she began to slip.

"What are ye doing here?" She held onto a branch, but in the moonlight Gregory could see her small hands begin to slide.

"*God's bones*! If yer brain wasn't so muddled with this foolish plan ye have, ye would ken why I am here."

"I have to leave before first light. Anthony is going to take me to The Gunn."

Gregory shook his head. "I think 'tis best if we stopped this conversation and get ye out of that tree before ye break yer fool neck."

"I'm slipping!" The words came out right before she dropped, hitting a branch which slowed her fall. She flailed her arms, trying to catch another branch.

"Just let go, Megan. I will catch ye." He barely got the words out before she landed in his arms. The surprise on her face must have matched the one on his.

He placed her on her feet. "What the devil were ye trying to do, lass? Ye could have killed yerself."

She brushed off her bodice and skirt. "Twould be better than having The Gunn kill me when he finds out I'm barren." She looked at him, her face as red as a beet. "I guess I should no' have blurted that out."

Gregory shrugged. Her confession was something he would think on later. Right now they had to leave as quickly as possible.

Megan turned to walk and fell to her knees.

He stopped and pulled her up. "What's wrong, lass?"

"I think when I hit the branch up there, I hurt my ankle."

"I'll take a look at it when we're away from here." In one quick motion, Gregory scooped her up in his arms, strode to where he'd left his horse.

"Wait! I need my satchel." She turned in his arms and pointed to the small bag she'd brought with her that had fallen from her hand when she tumbled from the tree.

Quickly, Gregory settled her on his horse, grabbed her bag, tossed it to her, swung his leg over the animal, settled Megan on his lap and rode off.

MEGAN WAS SO relieved at being rescued from her inane idea of climbing down the tree that any ill feelings she'd had for Gregory Mackenzie faded like a setting sun.

"Why did ye come back? I thought for sure ye'd be on yer way home right now."

The warrior grinned at her. "Dinna ya see the wink I left ye with?"

"Aye I did, but since I doona ken ye, I had no idea what it meant. Well, I mean, I did think that maybe it mean ye were no' really leaving, but then again I've had lads wink at me and—"

Gregory bent his head and took her mouth in a very interesting and voice-quieting kiss. She relaxed against him, the strength and warmth from his body giving her the best sense of calm and security she'd had since Robert's death. She knew in her heart that Gregory Mackenzie would not let her uncle drag her to The Gunn.

He raised his head, looking at her surprised face with a hint of laughter. "Keep in mind lass, every time ye're babbling like that I will quiet ye with a kiss."

Of course, she should be insulted, but based on her body's reaction to that very unexpected kiss, she might be doing a lot of babbling in the future.

They didn't ride far before she saw the men who had accompanied him on this mission sitting around a small fire, sipping on ale and talking. There were seven horses hobbled not too far from them.

She turned to Gregory. "Did ye bring an extra horse with ye?"

He grinned at her. "Nay, 'tis a Sinclair horse."

"Ye stole it?"

He laughed. "Aye." He looked at her, a glint in his eyes. "Just like I stole ye, too."

Gregory slid from the horse and wrapped his hands around Megan's waist and lifted her as if she weighed no more than a bag of feathers.

The men who had been sitting around the campfire kicked dirt on the low flames and headed to their horses. With her ankle still hurting, Gregory helped her over to one of the horses and settled her on the animal's back. "Do ye feel well enough to ride by yerself?"

Megan nodded and Gregory strode off, carrying her satchel which he fastened to his horse. He climbed on the animal and addressed the men. "We will ride through the night, but because of the darkness we will go slow. Once we have light we will pick up the pace. It won't take Anthony long to find out Lady Sinclair is missing and he will ken exactly who has her and the direction we're headed."

Gregory looked at her. "Lady Sinclair, I want ye to ride in the middle of our group. If the injury to yer ankle causes ye too much pain directing the horse yerself, let me know."

With those words, he raised his hand and turned toward the darkness. "We ride."

CHAPTER FIVE

MEGAN HAD STILL not recovered from her escape, and after riding hard and fast for many miles her heart was still thumping and her stomach cramped. She kept turning back waiting for Anthony and his crowd to come after them.

On the other hand, the way things were in the keep since Anthony had taken over after the old laird had died, no one would be sober enough to even know she was missing until well into the morning.

That also made her wonder why Anthony had said they were to leave at first light. She was certain the man hadn't seen first light since he'd been a lad.

"What are ye looking for, lass?" Gregory said as he dropped back from the front of the group to ride alongside her.

"Anthony, or The Gunn. I just doona believe I was able to get away from them so easily." She was tired from lack of sleep and growing sore from riding so hard and fast. The horse they'd stolen from the Sinclair keep was not the best one there.

"One of my men are about a mile behind us to watch for anyone coming after us. Ye need no' be concerned. I will take care of ye. No one will take ye away from me."

She wondered what he meant by that. They still had not settled the matter of her marrying him. She felt a need to honor Robert's request, but she was tired of men telling her who she should spend the rest of her life with.

First at a mere seventeen years she'd been sent to Robert, then before Robert was barely in his grave, Anthony had ordered that she marry The Gunn, and then Gregory Mackenzie showed up with a very old note about him marrying her.

All these things were wearing her down, and she noticed Gregory glancing at her from time to time. She sighed, not wanting to ask Gregory to stop for a break, but she would be forced to soon.

Almost as if he read her mind, he turned to her and said, "I think we will stop for a short while to give the horses a rest and a chance to drink." He waved in the direction in front of them to the east side. "There is a creek beyond the trees there."

He turned back to the other men. "We will stop here for a short break."

By their surprised expressions, they apparently were not used to breaks after such a short time, but she was grateful for Gregory's consideration.

He walked over to her horse and lifted her off. She got a strange feeling where his warm hands touched her. She looked at Gregory when he set her on the ground, and he studied her in an odd way.

She shook her head and turned to walk to the creek, but stumbled between the pain in her ankle and also where the inside of her legs had rubbed against the horse. Her entire miserable life from the past few weeks seemed to catch up with her. Tears came to her eyes and she tried very hard to wipe them before Gregory noticed.

Apparently, she had not been discreet enough because he wrapped his arm around her shoulder and pulled her close to his body. "I'm sorry ye have to go through this. If there was an easier way to get ye to Castle Leod, I would do it, but I am certain either Anthony or The Gunn or both will come after us."

She shivered, thinking about the life she would lead if The Gunn did end up catching them.

Gregory smiled down at her as she hobbled along to the

creek. "I can hear yer thoughts, Megan. Doona concern yerself with being caught." He turned her to him and face to face said, "Robert and I made that vow. I've never broken a vow in my life. Ye are safe. Believe that and trust me."

AS THEY MADE their way to the creek carefully in the dark, Gregory thought about what the lass had been through. They hadn't spoken enough to know what kind of marriage she'd had, what sort of husband Robert had been. Did her experience with marriage to Robert have to do with the reason she seemed so reluctant to marry again?

He took his time helping Megan to the creek. "I think if ye sit near the edge of the water and put yer sore foot in there, the coldness might help the pain."

If there was any coolness to be had, *he* certainly couldn't find it. Her soft, warm body, with the feel of all her curves against him was certainly not lowering his temperature.

Megan's scent of lavender and something else sweet reached his nose as he helped her settle on the ground, her sore foot free of stockings and shoe.

"With the sun rising, we're going to have to pick up our pace. I have every reason to believe Anthony and The Gunn are getting ready to ride now. Once ye've had enough time to ease yer foot, we'll have to go."

Megan's face turned a bright red. "I…um…" She cleared her throat. She lowered her head and spoke to her lap. "That is, there is something…"

Almost as if he'd been hit on the head, he realized her need to find a place to take care of her personal necessities. He looked around and spotted a small area with bushes, almost creating a shelter. He waved in that direction. "Ye can use the space over there."

She nodded and started to get up, her face reflecting the pain in her foot. "I think I will give ye my horse when we start up again. I suggest ye take my horse, Apex. He's a good horse who likes to work with his rider and not fight him. Then ye can sit easily and enjoy the ride, not spend yer time trying to get yer horse moving."

She seemed to breathe a sigh of relief. He reached out and helped her up and after picking up her stocking and shoe, gave up on watching her hobble and swung her into his arms.

"What are ye doing? Put me down."

He grinned at her red face and obvious agitation. "'Tis fine, lass. I hate to see ye in pain."

Gregory walked as close as he could to the bushes and let her down. He turned his back and she hobbled into the space. "Ye doona need to stand there, ye ken."

"'Tis fine. I doona have very good hearing anyway."

He laughed when she let out with a word he didn't think a young lass should know. But based on what Francis had said about the castle and the keep, it was no surprise.

After a whole lot of grumbling, Megan appeared. The poor lass looked exhausted.

"I've changed my mind, Megan. Ye will ride with me so ye can rest a bit."

Expecting an argument and getting none, he again scooped her up and headed to his horse. Once they were mounted, they took off at a faster pace. It was light out and Gregory knew it was only a matter of time before The Gunn set out for them.

What he didn't know was why Anthony was so adamant about marrying the lass off to The Gunn. There had to be something in it for him.

He was aware that arranged marriages took place all the time, but the rush for this one, with Robert's body barely settled in his grave, was questionable.

With Megan tucked comfortably in his lap, and him suffering a growing problem with a certain body part, he led the men to

Castle Leod.

"How long were ye and Robert married?" Gregory asked.

Megan yawned. "Almost two years. 'Twas an arranged marriage."

He didn't know why he asked the next question. "Were ye happy then?"

She shrugged. "I have nothing to compare it to. He spent his days on the list, training and working with the young lads. I helped run the keep until the old laird died, and instead of Robert taking his rightful place as laird, Anthony nudged him out of the role.

"I continued to do all the jobs I had been doing, but Robert spent less and less time doing what was considered his duty." She yawned again and looked at him directly. "'Twas a verra confusing time. When I asked Robert why he let Anthony make all the decisions about the clan, he just shrugged and said he was much better as a warrior than a laird."

She paused so long, he thought she had fallen asleep. Then in a very sleepy voice, she said, "Yet it was a minor battle that took his life."

Those were the last words spoken since Megan fell into a deep sleep. He cuddled her, trying to keep her warm.

He noticed in her rendition of Robert and their life at the keep, she never really spoke of their relationship together. She had blurted out earlier, probably by accident, that she was barren, so possibly that was a problem for the couple.

Barren. He never expected to marry, so the idea of children never mattered to him. If things worked out the way he had planned when he left Castle Leod, they would soon marry. Would he feel as though he'd been cheated if there were no children for him?

He was going over these things in his mind when Peter, the man he'd assigned to ride behind them, rode up. "The group is no more than five miles from us, Gregory."

He didn't need to ask him who he meant. He knew. They

were about to either engage in a battle, or escape. He looked down at Megan, sound asleep, and his decision was made.

"Lady Sinclair and I will ride a different route to Castle Leod. You will take her cloak, have one of the men put it on as a decoy and ride the way we had originally planned. We will meet ye at Castle Leod."

"Are ye sure that's a good idea, Gregory? Ye only have one horse. It will take longer to get where ye're going."

Gregory turned in another direction. "'Tis fine. Ye go ahead and do what we planned to foil Anthony's scheme." He looked down at a slumbering Megan. "I will take care of Lady Sinclair. 'Tis my duty."

CHAPTER SIX

’*T*IS MY DUTY.

The words resounded in her ears as Megan awoke from her nap and shifted in Gregory's arms. Just what she'd always wanted to be. Someone's duty. When she was told it was her duty to marry Robert Sinclair, she was angry. Lasses who didn't have a "duty" were able to marry the man of their choice. Someone to love and love her in return.

Robert turned out to be not a bad husband, but she never felt the connection between them that she had hoped to have in her marriage.

Then, with no bairns appearing, she couldn't help but wonder if Robert was annoyed having done his "duty". 'Twas never a conversation between them. She was not sure if he didn't want to speak about it or thought she didn't want to. By the time it had appeared to be an actual problem, Robert was dead and she was being told again what her "duty" was.

This time she had two duties. She was not sure what she thought of Gregory Makenzie, simply because there had been no time. So far, he seemed to be considerate of her, which eased her concerns somewhat.

He was also strong, handsome, and apparently honorable. But again, in his mind, this was *his duty*.

The other choice (not that she actually had one) was no

choice at all. She'd rather to have broken her neck in a fall from the tree than climb into the marriage bed with The Gunn.

She sat up when she saw her and Gregory break from the group and go in a different direction than the other warriors. "Why are we splitting up?"

He looked down at her and she felt something in her middle shift. A warm, strange feeling.

"My men and I had a plan that if those after ye got close enough to us, we would split up. We have a decoy with the other group which we hope will delay them for a while."

"Decoy?"

He grinned. "Aye. While ye slept we took yer cloak from yer satchel and gave it to one of the warriors to wear. We're hoping they are fooled long enough for us to get away from them. Also our route is not well known and it should take them time to figure it out."

"How long will it take for us to arrive at Castle Leod?"

Gregory shrugged. "'Tis hard to say. The other way would have been four or five days. This way will add another one or possibly two to our trip depending on how the weather holds out. We still have a bit of summer left, but there is always rain to delay us if the ground gets too sloppy."

Suddenly aware of how cuddled up she was to Gregory, she shifted. The man brought out strange feelings in her body and she didn't have the energy to examine them now.

AFTER A FEW minutes, Gregory asked, "What was yer job in the keep?"

They'd been so busy arguing with the Sinclair, and then being thrown out of the castle, resulting in him rescuing Megan from their hold, that they hadn't spent any time learning about each other.

Her eyes lit up, which told him that part of her life there was satisfying.

"I helped the chatelaine quite a bit when the old laird was alive. Then after he died and Anthony pushed Robert out of his laird's position, he relegated me to working in the kitchen with the other maids."

That was certainly not an answer he would have expected. Didn't Robert step in and remove his wife from kitchen duties?

"Did ye like working in the kitchen?"

She shrugged. "'Twasn't so verra hard. I got to ken a few of the maids and made a few friends."

"If ye had yer choice, what job would ye like at Castle Leod?"

Megan smiled. "I'm sure Lady Mackenzie would decide on that, but if I was given a choice, I would love to do healing. 'Tis what I did at my home with my mam before she passed away and then I was married off to Robert."

"Castle Leod is quite large and it seems the warriors— especially the newer ones—are always getting injured. I'm sure Emma could use yer help."

"She is yer healer now?"

"Aye. A sweet lass. Ye would like her."

A few minutes passed, and then Gregory asked again, "Were ye happy in yer marriage?"

He didn't know why but felt himself tensing as he waited for her answer.

She offered him a soft smile. "Is any marriage happy?"

He shrugged his shoulders. "I doona ken since it has ne'er been my wish to marry."

She snorted. "But here ye are dragging me to yer clan to marry me." She looked up at him. "As yer *duty*."

He had a feeling he hadn't said the right thing and needed to figure out how to answer the lass without making it seem that he had no liking or desire for her.

He did. Her golden red hair cascading down her back, deep green eyes and enough curves to keep a man happy would certainly be a lass to desire. But did he like her? Would he want her as a wife if he didn't have the duty to marry her? He didn't really know her. That was the reason for asking questions. She was quite evasive in her answers, which he found troubling.

"I would be lying to ye lass if I said nay, I'm not here because of duty since we both ken that is the verra reason I showed up at the Sinclair castle." He stopped for a moment and added, "Ye have to allow that marriage was never something I planned on."

She lifted her chin and stared him right in the eye, even with the horse going at a clip. "Then why did ye agree to the pledge to marry each other's widows? Did ye no' take it seriously?"

Gregory stiffened at her charge. "We were young lads; neither one of us expected to die until we were of an old age. In fact, I ne'er thought about fulfilling the duty"—he cringed at using that word—"because Robert was such a good warrior that I thought he would definitely live longer than me."

She stared at him for a moment and then shook her head. "What a surprise for ye." She turned and left him wondering if their conversation had been good or bad for whatever relationship they were headed toward.

GREGORY THOUGHT THEY'D traveled a fair distance considering the horse carried both of them. They'd been quiet since the conversation earlier. Not one to banter back and forth with a lass—or anyone for that matter—he had no problem with the silence.

The sun was beginning to set and except for some dried meat he had on him, they'd had nothing to sustain them besides that and water.

Megan looked like she was about to collapse. He knew he should not have pushed them so far, but since he was the only one protecting the lass, he preferred not to encounter the Gunn or the Sinclair men.

"We'll stop for the night now."

She sighed and looked up at him. "Thank ye. Verra, verra

much."

What was it about the lass that made him feel guilty? As if she was suffering and he allowed it. Another strike for marriage. He knew nothing about providing a woman comfort, talking to her, saying the right things.

If he intended to fulfill his vow, he had to learn all of that. The last thing he wanted to do was make the lass miserable for the rest of her life.

He knew he was the better choice for her to marry, but when one considered who the other choice was, it was not really a compliment to him.

MEGAN SLID OFF the horse into Gregory's arms. His strong, muscular arms. Even after hours of riding, he appeared as if he could go for another few hours.

Not her. She was so grateful when they stopped that she almost cried. She knew just by the short time they'd been traveling that Gregory Mackenzie knew very little about women. She imagined him staring at her with wide eyes if she broke down and cried.

"Why doona ye gather some sticks and we will start a fire. While ye'er doing that, I'll see what I can find for our meal."

Megan nodded and began her chore as he walked off with his bow and arrow as well as his dirk strapped to his leg. She was so tired it seemed as though she was the horse that had carried them part of the night and all day.

She'd been so busy thinking about the past few years and what she was headed to now, that she never paid attention to their travels.

The area they were in was best called a deer path. The dappled fading sunlight on the leaves was beautiful. The air was now getting cooler, and soon autumn would turn into colder air and the Highland snow of winter. She shivered at the thought.

As she gathered sticks for their fire, small animals scurried about, maybe looking for something for their suppers. She had plenty of wood, but had no idea how to turn it into a fire. She wrapped her arms around herself, wishing to have her cloak back.

The sound of thrashing in the wooded area caught her attention. Gregory moved aside some branches and walked toward her.

"I'm sorry I dinna start a fire, but I'm afraid I doona ken how to do it without a flint."

Gregory dropped three rabbits at her feet and withdrew a flint from his pouch and tossed it to her.

She caught it and started the fire as he cut the rabbits and skinned them.

Megan pushed the wood around with a stick. "I have a question for ye."

He continued with his cutting. "What?"

"Are ye truly trying to save me, or win a contest against Robert's uncle?"

Never looking up he said, "Both."

CHAPTER SEVEN

I T HAD BEEN a rough night for the two of them. After Gregory had the rabbits skinned, Megan had looked as though she was ready to drop to the ground.

He tossed one of the rabbits to her after shoving it on a stick. "Yer supper."

She jumped and glowered at him. "Verra funny."

"If ye want to eat, ye have to work."

She shoved the rabbit into the fire. "I have no intention of no' doing my share. I'll have ye ken I am a verra hard worker." She nodded to the animal at her feet. "I can skin and cook a rabbit."

Gregory grinned, enjoying her annoyance. He had no idea why he did that. 'Twas possible he was trying to keep himself from feeling anything for the lass besides duty. He still wasn't sure he would not turn into his da once wed.

He would never want to see the pain on Megan's face each morning as he disappointed her. As far as putting his hands on her, he would cut them off before he would do that.

Since they'd given away her cloak to use as a decoy, Gregory wrapped both of them with his plaid once they were ready to sleep. He had a hard time with Megan and her soft warm body right next to him, but the poor lass was so tired that she had barely laid her head down when she fell asleep.

The next morning, wrapped around each other like two

puppies, they arose with the sun, packed up and left. The air was chillier than it had been the day before and the threatening clouds gathering had him wondering how much distance they would be able to cover this day.

Gregory wrapped himself and Megan in his plaid again, cursing the decision he'd made to use her cloak as a decoy. She was tempting enough when he was just speaking with her, but having her against his body, not sleeping, but very much awake with her heart beating next to his and all her warm softness and tempting curves pressed up against him made Gregory want to throw the plaid off.

The weather held up for most of the day, but the clouds grew thicker and more threatening the closer they got to sundown.

Before Gregory thought it best to stop for the night, the first of very large and very cold raindrops began to fall. The longer they continued to ride, the more Megan's body shook.

So far he had not seen any spot where he would be comfortable with both of them sleeping. He was somewhat familiar with the area and knew there was an abandoned half-collapsed bothy only about a mile or so away. Fortunately, it was in the direction they were headed.

"C-c-can we st-stop soon?" Megan looked up at him with pathetic eyes. His stomach muscles cramped at the sight and he got the ridiculous feeling to hold her even more tightly.

"Aye," he said, rather abruptly to chase away the feelings he did not want.

She stiffened and turned to face forward. She moved a bit so she no longer rested against him. He reminded himself that keeping them from forming any type of connection was a good thing.

MEGAN HAD NO idea why Gregory was so thoughtful and kind

one minute then throwing bloody rabbits at her and showing a great deal of annoyance because she asked to stop. He was definitely a difficult man.

She sighed. Hopefully once they escaped Anthony and The Gunn they could get this fake marriage over with and go their own ways. She was certain there was plenty at Castle Leod to keep her busy. Gregory being the Second in Command to the Mackenzie laird he would most likely be very busy himself training new warriors. Hopefully since she'd already blurted out that she was barren he would not require her to share his bed. Robert's attentions had seemed to diminish long before she went almost two years without any bairns.

Since she'd never really enjoyed the marriage bed the way she heard the maids speak of it, she figured there was something wrong with her, which was why she'd never produced a bairn.

Having no mam to talk to her about such things, when the time grew closer to when she was to marry Robert she blushingly asked her da what to expect. He brushed her off, redder in the face than she was and said her husband would take care of that.

Gregory pulled on the horse's reins. Between the heavy clouds, drenching rain, and setting sun, she barely made out a small bothy in front of them. It didn't look too sturdy, but with her body growing wetter and colder every minute, she didn't care as long as it had a roof.

Gregory jumped from the horse and wrapped his hands around her waist, setting her on the ground. "Go inside. 'Tis not a lot of protection, but better than nothing."

She nodded and made her way slowly and carefully to the space. The cold air was already turning the rain on the ground to ice. She felt as though she would never be warm again.

"See if we're lucky and if there is dry wood inside. Nothing out here would be able to burn."

Megan nodded and entered the bothy. There was, indeed, a fireplace with wood in it, and more stacked to the side. Mayhap hunters used it on occasion. For whatever reason that the wood was here, all she cared about was getting out of the cold rain.

Gregory entered the space with the bag he carried on his horse as well as her satchel. He withdrew a dry plaid and handed it to her. "Ye will need to remove yer clothes and wrap yerself with this while I make a fire."

Her eyes grew wide. "Take off all my clothes?"

He didn't turn toward her, but squatted in front of the fireplace and used his flint to start a fire. "Aye."

"What will I wear?"

He turned back, a grin on his face. "The plaid I just gave ye."

She opened her mouth and shut it a few times before she cleared her throat. "Will ye stay in yer wet clothes, then?"

He returned his attention to the fire. "Nay, we will share the plaid and place the wet one in front of the fire to dry."

⇢⇥⇤⇠

GREGORY GRINNED AT the grumbling coming from the lass. She might be grumbling, but he was sweating in spite of the cold. Once the fire was going, he pulled out left-over rabbit meat and warmed it.

'Twas going to be a difficult night for sure.

"'Twill be alright, Megan. We will sleep back-to-back with the plaid wrapped around both of us. Nothing need happen that ye doona want to happen."

She huffed. "That is a verra indistinct statement." She continued to eat the rabbit, wrapped in the plaid that she now learned would be shared with Gregory. And no clothes on!

Since he was still dressed, Gregory went outside to take care of his needs and get water from the overflowing creek behind them. The rain had stopped, but the night darkness with clouds still in the sky made it hard to see. He would have to walk with Megan so she could take care of her own needs.

He laughed thinking about how she would handle that.

When he returned to the bothy, she was still wrapped in the plaid, curled up in front of the hearth. She had tossed the bones from the rabbits into the fire.

"I assume ye will want to take care of yer needs outside?"

She nodded and stood, the large plaid dragging on the ground. "I will be right back."

He reached out and grabbed her arm. The plaid slipped and she quickly grasped it, the other side sliding. She flushed as she did her best to wrap the plaid around her body.

"Nay, ye will no' go outside by yerself, lass. 'Tis dark out there and ye could verra well trip and fall on the slippery ground."

Her jaw dropped. "Ye canno' go with me!"

He stood. "Aye I can and I will." Without any further comments, he grabbed her arm and marched her toward the opening. She wrestled with the plaid and glowered at him.

The ground was more slippery than when he'd gone out since the temperature had continued to drop. They made it to where she was able to take care of her needs, and he took her arm and helped her back.

Megan was shivering something fierce when they returned to the bothy. Thankfully, the fire was still going strong, but he wasn't sure it would continue through the night. It appeared they might only have each other to keep warm which would be dangerous if it was closer to winter.

She sat by the fire and settled the plaid around her. Gregory stayed seated while he removed the rest of his clothes. "We will need to re-arrange the plaid so it covers us both."

She didn't acknowledge him, but merely nodded. With her back to him, she said, "Go ahead and do what ye need to do so I can get some sleep."

He grinned at the sharpness in her voice.

It took a few minutes for Megan to move off the plaid and cover both of them. She turned away from him and he slid closer to her so they shared their warmth without facing each other.

'Twas an awkward way to sleep but with Megan being so skittish they had no choice.

Morning came faster than Gregory thought it would considering what he'd had to endure.

Once he awoke, he lay perfectly still as he glanced down at their bodies. He was on his back and Megan was sprawled all over him, her head on his chest and her leg thrown over his.

Her golden red hair flowed down her back and over his shoulders like a waterfall of color. Her beautiful breasts pressed against him and his hand had wandered during the night to cup her lush bottom.

He groaned when his member stood up and saluted "good morning" to the lass.

Right before she sat up and screamed.

CHAPTER EIGHT

MEGAN JUMPED UP, tugging on the plaid, pulling it complete-ly off Gregory, and then, shocked at seeing his naked body, threw it at him, leaving herself naked. Then, looking down at her own body she attempted to cover everything with her hands.

Gregory couldn't help it. He burst out laughing. "What the devil're ye doing lass?"

"We're naked!"

"Aye. We took our clothes off last night. Doona ye remember?"

She hurried over to the clothes laying in front of the fire and quicky found her pieces and dressed herself. She headed to the opening at the front of the bothy.

Gregory struggled into his clothes. "Wait, Megan. Where are ye going?"

"Outside. To the bushes." As she turned to him, her face was once again bright red.

"Nay. Wait for me. I canno' let ye go outside alone. Did ye forget we're being tracked?"

She took a deep breath, and now with them both dressed, seemed a bit more relaxed. "Nay I dinna forget, I just didn't think."

"'Ye have to think, lass. We are still in danger, even though we split up from the others. Once our pursuers catch up to them, they will immediately ken what we did and try to find the path we took."

"Will they find out from yer men?"

He grinned. "Nay. If they try to engage my well-trained warriors with the idea of getting information from them they will ne'er find us because they will all be dead."

Gregory took her arm to help her over the wet ground and roots.

As much as he believed that she would have liked to do without his help, she gripped his arm as her foot started to slip out from under her.

"Ye are pretty confident of yer men's abilities."

"Aye."

He stood alongside the bushes, his back to her while she did what she needed to do. He decided to return her to the bothy where she was relatively safe before he took care of his own needs.

"Do we have food?" she asked as they walked back.

"Nay. But there is a small village no' far from here where we can get a meal."

"Is that safe?"

He shrugged "If we are careful."

Once she was settled back in the bothy he told her that when he was finished, they would leave.

WHILE MEGAN WAITED for Gregory to return, she made sure the fire was out, grateful that there had been enough wood to last the night. She spent time outside, but not too far from the bothy, gathering more wood that she could carry to replace what they had used. Then she fumbled through her satchel and tried her best to clean her teeth and brush her hair into some semblance of order.

She would ask Gregory to make one more walk with her to the creek so she could wash her hands and face.

While she waited, anxious to get away from where they were and to a real village, she thought of the man and how 'twas possible he would end up her husband. The quick glance she'd gotten of his muscular body was enough to have her both nervous and excited to see if the marriage bed with him was different from Robert's.

Then she felt guilty. Robert had not been a bad husband. He was just more interested in his warrior training and visiting the ale house in town than he was with her. That could very well have been her fault, since as a barren woman she probably held little appeal.

If he hadn't been killed they would probably have had a long, boring marriage. Was there any reason for her to believe life with Gregory Mackenzie would be any different?

He was second-in-command to Laird Mackenzie so he obviously had a great deal of training to do. As she'd told Gregory earlier, she would be content to do whatever job Lady Mckenzie assigned to her, but would love to continue to learn more about healing.

What was confusing was why seeing his body had her now questioning her earlier thoughts about having him go his way and she go hers. Robert had had a warrior's body also, but she had been annoyed that he went his own way all the time.

'Twas a strange thing.

Gregory stepped into the space carrying a sack of water. "I use this to drink from when there is no cup available. I thought ye might want some."

Megan stood. "Actually, besides a drink of water I could use some of it to wash my face and hands."

He handed her the sack and nodded. "While ye do that I will see to the horse."

She nodded and proceeded to drink first, then used what was

left to wash her hands and face. Feeling refreshed, she waited for Gregory to return. Her stomach growled, reminding herself of the promise to find a real meal.

"We're ready to leave," Gregory said.

Megan stepped outside, happy to see sunshine. She glanced at Gregory who scooped her up and placed her on the horse. He swung up behind her and after making sure she was wrapped with the plaid and settled, he urged his horse into motion and they were off.

Happy with the fair day and the idea of a real meal, she found herself smiling for the first time in days.

"I can feel yer smile from here," Gregory said.

She turned to see him grinning at her. Again, her stomach fluttered and something strange happened to her woman's parts. Something she'd rarely felt before.

It might have been the bright sunlight, or her brief sense of happiness, but Gregory seemed even more handsome to her today.

He must have used the creek to wash his face and dampen his hair. His blue eyes looked even more brilliant since he was really looking at her. Her breath caught and she looked away, then shifted. There was no good to be had in developing a fancy for the man.

He would never feel the same since he was marrying her to fulfill a duty.

THE VILLAGE WAS larger than Megan had assumed. Various shops lined the two streets that faced the village green. Butcher, greengrocer, baker, shoemaker, blacksmith, tailor, and a carpenter were as much as she could see as they made their way into the village stable.

Once they left the horse with instructions to brush him down and feed him, Gregory took her hand and they stepped into the bright sunlight.

"Ah, just what I was looking for," he said, waving toward the end of the line of shops. A nice size building faced them, with the words: "The Ram's Head," on a large painted sign hanging over the door.

As if to emphasize his comment, his stomach let out with growl. It seemed they were both in need of decent food.

The alehouse was dark and the smoke from the fireplace, because of the small chimney, was unable to leave the building, giving the place a very hazy appearance.

Gregory placed his hand on her lower back and directed her to a table in the corner.

"My, 'tis dark in here. Shouldn't we find another table?" Megan asked, looking around. The smoke was already burning her eyes.

"Nay." He pulled out a chair for her. "We're in hiding, remember? I rarely turn my back to the door when I'm somewhere unfamiliar. And knowing one of Gunn's or Sinclair's men could stop in here, I prefer to see him before he sees me."

Megan shivered and ran her palms up and down her arms. "I hope the food is good."

Just then a young lass approached them. "Good day to ye. What can I get for ye?"

Gregory looked over at Megan.

"Do ye have cider?"

The girl smiled. "Nay. Only drinks we have are ale and whisky."

What she could use was a hot cup of tea. But that wasn't an option. "I'll have an ale."

"Ye can bring me an ale also. What are ye serving today?"

Megan felt a sense of something strange when she saw Gregory offer his best smile at the girl who returned his smile until Megan was ready to smack her face.

Whatever was wrong with her?

"We're still serving breakfast. We have eggs, bacon, ham, tatties, and black pudding."

"I'll have it all," Gregory said. Another bright smile.

She wanted to kick him. "The eggs, ham, and tatties for me," Megan said coolly.

The lass nodded and left them. Megan looked over at Gregory, feeling as though she should say something. "I doona care for black pudding."

He grinned. "No' everyone does."

Within minutes, the lass set down the two mugs of ale and two plates of food. She stepped back and said, "Ye look like good people, ye ken?"

What was this lass about?

Gregory leaned back in his chair, crossed his arms and frowned. "Aye."

She moved closer. "Early this morning, there was a mon in here looking for a mon and lass traveling together. The description he gave is verra similar to ye."

Gregory nodded and picked up his fork. "Thank ye lass."

She walked off and Gregory nodded at Megan. "Eat up lass. We need to be on our way."

CHAPTER NINE

E VEN THOUGH MEGAN was concerned that either Gunn or her uncle were on their trail, she was not scared enough to skip her breakfast. Gregory also asked the tavern lass if she could make them a couple of sandwiches to take with them.

Megan thought that was a wonderful idea since she had little desire to stop at another village if whoever was after her was that close.

"How do ye suppose they caught up to us so soon?" Megan asked as they reached the village stable.

Gregory threw her over the horse's back, handed her the sack of food and climbed up behind her. "I doona ken. Mayhap Gunn's men have an exceptional tracker with them."

"'Tis only my opinion, but from what I've seen, if there is only one mon after us, he would be no threat to ye."

Gregory leaned forward to look her in the face. He grinned. "What does that mean?"

She shrugged her shoulders, her face tingling so that she knew it was turning a tad red. "Um, only that I think ye would win just about any fight ye got into."

The fool mon laughed out loud, probably scaring the small animals in the woods. "Ye think so, lass? So ye think I can beat just about anyone?"

"Oh, stop it." She turned forward and pulled the plaid around her shoulders. "The last thing ye need are more ways to add to yer arrogance."

He continued to chuckle so long she thought about hitting him with sack of food they carried, but it wasn't strong enough to do anything to his hard head.

In spite of his laughter, Gregory seemed to grow more tense as they rode off. She picked up on it and, now aware of every sound, felt her muscles tighten. They rode like that for the entire morning until Gregory said, "We need to stop. The horse needs a break or we won't make the entire trip."

Megan nodded, grateful for a chance to ease her muscles. Gregory led the horse to another creek. He jumped off and wrapped his hands around her waist, placing her on the ground. He stared at her for a minute, his blue eyes saying something she didn't understand. Then after brushing the hair off her face, he cupped her cheeks and lowered his mouth to hers.

Startled at first, she tensed up again, but then relaxed against his warm body. He tilted her head and nudged her lips. She opened and he swept in, touching and stroking with his tongue. When she moaned he placed his large hands on her lower back and pulled her close.

In his arms, it was difficult to remember why she was not happy to marry him. He was strong, protective, intelligent, and handsome.

It is my duty.

She pushed those words away as different parts of her body woke up and things she'd never felt before raised her temperature so she no longer needed the wrap.

Gregory pulled away and placed his hands on her shoulders. "Ye kiss fine, lass."

She grinned. "So do ye."

He led the horse to the creek and Megan followed them.

Robert had never given her any sort of a compliment. 'Twas probably because he found her wanting when it came to bedding her.

She knelt on the ground, scooped up the clear, cold water and drank. She also gave herself a quick face and hand wash to refresh herself.

Gregory squatted alongside her. "I doona ken who the mon was looking for us in the village, but I have a verra good suspicion 'twas one of Gunn's men."

"I thought this was an unknown path?"

"Nay. 'Tis no' verra unknown but few travelers use it because it takes ye away from the main road in such a way that it adds time to yer trip. Also there is a mountain pass that a lot of people want to avoid. Most prefer the better known paths to Castle Leod."

He looked up at the sky and then turned to her. "Just so ye ken lass, in a short time we will reach that mountain pass. I've been over it many times, but it's verra narrow and ye need to stay as still as ye can while we're crossing."

"Is it dangerous?" Megan asked.

Gregory smiled. "Life is dangerous, lass." He immediately regretted his words, thinking about Megan's recent loss.

She ignored his comment, which made him wonder once again about her marriage to the man he thought he knew so well.

He took his turn drinking from the creek, thinking about the mountain cross coming up. It wasn't long, maybe two miles. But he had to keep his concentration for them to make it safely to the end. From there it would be a very short ride to the castle. Maybe just one more day.

In thinking about the crossing, he had considered wrapping a cloth around Megan's eyes, since the first time crossing the path could be frightening. He wasn't sure if she'd be insulted or happy to do it.

They both took a turn in the bushes and then Gregory tossed Megan up on his horse.

"Ye ken, ye throw me on the animal like I'm sack of flour."

She scowled as she straightened her dress.

He gave her that smile again that she oftentimes dreamed

about. "Believe me, Megan I think of ye in many ways, but ne'er as a sack of flour."

There was no conversation between them until Gregory pulled on the horse's reins and stopped. "We are getting close to the mountain pass."

Megan nodded.

"'Tis yer decision but I can cover yer eyes if ye think it would make it easier for ye."

"Nay. I will be fine." She wasn't sure she would be fine, but felt a little silly having him wrap a cloth around her head like she was a bairn.

He made sure she was settled comfortably and securely placed on the horse and then started forward. They were less than a quarter mile when Megan turned in his arms, scaring him to death since he thought she was falling. She wrapped her arms around him and leaned her head on his chest. He could hear her whimpering, but said nothing, merely pulling her closer.

Gregory was used to traveling over the area, but he was always very careful since it wasn't a smart idea to take the ride for granted.

The horse stopped for a minute and Megan hugged him closer.

"'Tis all right, lass. Not much longer."

She whimpered again.

"Ye're doing great, Megan. Just hold on."

Once they reached the end of the pass, Gregory said, "We're back on solid ground."

She released him and took a deep breath. "I would no' want to do that verra often."

"There is no reason to. We will stop for a little while and give us and the horse a chance to rest."

When he lifted her off, he noticed she was shaking. Once she was firmly on the ground, he pulled her close again. "Ye were verra brave, lass."

To his astonishment, she burst into tears. He walked her over to a tree stump where they both sat. He pulled her onto his lap. "'Tis o'er. I will ne'er let any harm come to ye."

She looked up at him, the tears still clumped on her eyelashes. "Because 'tis yer duty."

He didn't like that she kept referring to his "duty". Aye, there was no doubt that was why he arrived at the Sinclair's. But the more time he spent with her, the less he concerned himself with his duty to her.

Megan was a smart, pretty, and strong lass. Whatever her relationship had been with her husband, from things she'd said, he had reason to believe it hadn't been ideal. While he and Robert had been friends and training partners, they never discussed their personal lives. It had surprised him at the time they made their vow that he would even think of doing such a thing.

He leaned forward and kissed her on the top of her head. "'Twas my duty to fetch ye as Robert and I promised to each other, but it could be more if we both give it a chance."

He was surprised by his own words. Could it be more if they both gave it a chance? He'd never wanted to marry and therefore be responsible for anyone other than himself, to have an obligation to make someone else happy. Especially a woman, one whom he found very confusing at times.

And children. He shook his head. His da had been a bad example. Would it be a "like father, like son" situation for him and Megan?

She looked up at him. "Tell me something about Robert. He wasn't one to spend much time with me. I doona even ken if he was happy in our marriage. Our fathers made the arrangements and once we married, it almost seemed to me that Robert had no intention of changing anything about his life."

She swung her legs back and forth like a bairn. "I feel like a horse or another animal, passed from one person to the next without any care for what I want."

"I'm sorry ye feel that way, but 'tis the way of the world. Women must be protected and cared for, and 'tis a man's—" he hesitated, and she said,

"Duty."

He nodded slowly and dragged out the word. "Ayyyee."

They stared into the distance for a bit and then said, "I have a story or two about yer husband." He grinned at her.

She shifted and gave him her full attention, hoping it wasn't something that would upset her. Something about another lass.

"He was a better warrior in training than I was. Stronger, quicker. One time while training, I received a hard blow and landed flat on my back. I was embarrassed, especially when the others in training with us laughed.

"However, Robert walked over to me and pulled me up and turned to the others and said, 'Doona make fun of a fellow warrior. We train as one and we fight as one. If a warrior needs more training, we should give it to him and encourage him. Do ye want a weak swordsman at yer back on the battlefield?'"

Megan grinned. "He said that?"

"Aye. And he meant it. From that day on, I received extra training from the others and even when I was ready to drop, he kept pushing me."

"It sounds as if he was a true friend."

Gregory nodded.

CHAPTER TEN

S HE DIDN'T REACT to the story, but it was good to hear about Robert from someone else's experience. He was always protective of her, but she had seen it as a way to control her without giving her the softer attention that a woman craved.

Gregory had certainly given her something to think about. He placed her on her feet and stood. "I think 'tis time to continue. There is another village we should reach by the late afternoon. We can get a meal there, also and even get room to sleep in."

"That sounds wonderful!" She grasped his hand and attempted to pull him up. "Let us leave."

The village was smaller than the one they had stopped at before. The alehouse was not as large either, but Megan was still grateful to be out of the woods, off the mountain pass, and with any luck have a hot meal. And maybe even a bed!

She noticed that Gregory took his time entering the village area, looking around carefully. Most likely he was concerned that whoever had been asking for them in the other village was here waiting for them.

"We will have a meal and see if we can get a room for the night," he said as he handed the horse over to the stable lad.

"Stay close to me," he continued. "I'm no' sure how safe it is for us." He reached out and took her hand in his. His large, warm hand. Again she felt the tingling from their contact. She had never noticed that with her husband. It was both frightening and exciting.

She glanced at him out of the corner of her eye. Yes, he was definitely handsome, and possessed a strong warrior's body. There was no doubt he presented himself to anyone interested that he was someone who could protect her.

Her thoughts wandered as they made their way to the alehouse. Thoughts about the words that Gregory had said before. Did she think, as he'd mentioned, that they could have more if they gave it a chance?

No. If she allowed him into her heart she would be disappointed when he grew tired of her and began to look elsewhere for a "real" woman to warm his bed, not some barren woman who held no appeal.

She was almost certain Robert had been dissatisfied enough with her to do the same. She didn't need to put herself through that again. Although she would always be grateful for Gregory rescuing her from Anthony's plans, it would still be better for her to remember she was his "duty" and not look for more than what she had with Robert.

The alehouse was smaller, but not as smoky as the last one. Again, Gregory led them to the table at the back of the room, right next to a door most likely leading to the outside of the building.

A young lass approached them, swinging her hips and smiling at Gregory, ignoring her. "Good evening. What can I get for ye?" She pursed her lips, most likely thinking she looked available. Which she did.

And probably was.

"An ale for me." He looked over at Megan. "What do ye want, wife?"

Annoyed, Megan snapped. "I will have an ale, also."

The lass wandered off, after giving Gregory a smile and more swinging of her hips.

Megan frowned. "Why did ye call me 'wife'?"

He shrugged. "Because I doona trust anyone here and dinna want to give the lass any encouragement."

Although she was pleased with his comments, she couldn't help but think like Robert, Gregory would most likely look elsewhere when he grew tired of her being barren. Megan huffed. "As if having a wife would stop most men from accepting her obvious invitation."

Gregory's brows rose and he stared at her. "No' me. I would ne'er do that. Marriage is no' something to have when ye want it but ignore when ye doona want it."

Megan studied him as they waited for the lass to return. Was this truly a man who honored his marriage vows? Could she feel comfortable with him, confident that he was not searching for other women so he could warm their beds?

The lass returned to their table with the two mugs of ale. If she bent over Gregory any farther her lady parts would fall out of her dress, right into his face.

He merely nodded at her and once the lass had left, he turned to Megan. "I also called ye 'wife' because I intend for us to stay in the same room."

"Why?"

"Protection. I cannot keep ye safe if ye'er in another room. And no' just from those who might be looking for us. These small alehouses are often filled with less than savory men belonging to no clan and causing trouble wherever they go."

Megan grinned. "Ye do ken that saying I was yer wife in front of a witness automatically married us? And sharing a room just makes it a consummated marriage?"

Gregory offered her a smile that she was sure got many a young lass into his bed. It warmed up her insides, especially in certain places. "Then we don't need to worry about Gunn coming after ye if we're already married."

Before she could think on that, the lass returned and leaned up against Gregory, laying her hand on his arm. "Will ye be eating tonight?" She licked her lips.

He shifted a bit to separate them, moving so her hand slid from him. "Aye. What is yer special today?"

She threw her long hair over her shoulder and grinned, placing one hand on her hip. "Me."

God's bones, if the lass was any more forward she would be pulling Gregory up by his hair and dragging him off.

No longer willing to put up with her, Megan said, "My *husband* and I will have whatever the special *from the kitchen* is." She paused and waved her hand in a dismissal. "Not ye."

Megan turned back to Gregory and smiled, taking a sip of her ale.

The lass huffed off.

GREGORY ALMOST CHOKED on his drink. Megan Sinclair was no one to fool with. She might be a sweet-looking lass, but apparently underneath all that sweetness was a woman of steel.

His opinion of her was certainly changing. She might shake and weep with fear crossing the mountain pass, but his sweet-looking wife surprised him, again.

More than once he wondered what her marriage had been like. Things she told him sounded like she was not very happy. It appeared Robert was not faithful to his marriage vows and other things she said made him believe theirs was not a strong relationship.

Hopefully, the story he'd told her about Robert would show the lass a different sort of man than the one she knew. Given what seemed to have been her experience so far, it was no wonder the lass was not too eager to marry again.

If she agreed to really wed him once they arrived at Castle Leod, since he knew Beth Mackenzie would insist on a proper wedding, he might not wish to give his heart away. He would certainly protect her, provide for her and never embarrass her by seeking other women to warm his bed.

Once they finished their meal and he made certain the lass who continued to drape herself all over him finally realized he was not interested in a tumble with her, he secured a room from the innkeeper, then he and Megan made their way upstairs.

"Oh, my," Megan said as she looked around the sparse area.

Oh my, indeed. The only good thing to be said about the room was it provided a roof over their heads in case of a rainstorm, and a bed big enough for maybe one person. A very small person, he thought, as he dropped his sack and placed his hands on his hips and looked around the scant quarters.

Megan looked up at him, chewing her lip. "Where will we sleep?"

Gregory held in his grin as he waved toward the bed. "Right there."

She sucked in a breath. "On top of each other?"

"Aye. I'm afraid so, lass. With no fire, 'tis too cold to sleep anywhere else."

She studied the bed and looked back and forth between the two of them, then shrugged. "'Tis afraid I am that ye are right."

His body reacted immediately to her instant consent. The thought of her soft body and gentle curves resting on top of him all night had him thinking that sleeping on the floor might not be a bad idea. Accidental marriage or not, he doubted Megan would consider it just fine to enjoy the consummation of words spoken in front of a witness.

She sat on the bed and smirked at him. "Mayhap yer friend downstairs has a larger bed she would be willing to share with ye."

Gregory pulled her into his arms and placed his knuckle under her chin, raising her eyes up to meet his. "I hope ye are joking, lass. I was no' just spewing words when I said I would ne'er share another woman's bed, especially one who I am certain has probably worn out more than one mattress."

Megan laughed. "I believe ye are right."

"'Tis cold in here, so we will need to keep our clothes on, and I'll wrap my plaid around us."

He hoped she would not bring up the idea of less clothing being warmer than no clothes as he'd told her before when their clothes were soaked. He didn't think he could do that again and get through the night without convincing Megan to consummate this accidental marriage.

Although he didn't think of himself as any great seducer of women, based on what he'd seen from Megan so far, he knew it wouldn't take much effort on his part.

Since it was late and he wanted an early start in the morning, he removed his boots and climbed onto the bed, his plaid in his hand ready to toss over them. Once he was comfortable—or as comfortable as he would be for the rest of the night, he held out his hand. "Come here, Megan. 'Tis growing late."

She took a deep breath and nodded. She untied her boots and stood alongside the bed. "Mayhap side by side would work better?"

"We can certainly try it." He moved over and she climbed in alongside him, and promptly fell to the floor.

"Nay. I'll sleep on the outside," Gregory said and hopped off the bed. Megan made her way over to the edge of the bed and banged her head against the wall. There still wasn't enough room for half his body.

"Lass, ye're going to injury yerself. I'll end up squashing ye like a bug during the night. One on top of the other is the best way."

She was off the bed again and he laid down, then held in the groan once she climbed onto him. He started counting numbers as she wiggled around before she settled.

"Are ye finished, lass?" He knew his voice came out sharp, but he was struggling.

"Aye." She rested her head on his chest and he wrapped the plaid around them.

He had counted up into the tens of thousands before he finally drifted off.

CHAPTER ELEVEN

GREGORY WOULD HAVE preferred to sleep on the mountain pass than next to Megan again. Unless it was in a real bed with both of them naked. That, he would welcome.

He'd been awake for some time, but Megan slept on. Moving and moving and moving. He was ready to pull off all their clothes and be done with it.

He reached up and pushed her hair off her face. "Lass. 'Tis time to wake up."

She slowly opened her eyes, heavy with sleep, and offered him an unhurried, sultry smile. He placed his hands behind her head and took her mouth in a kiss of complete possession.

He felt passion in her that he doubted Robert had ever discovered. No woman who looked like Megan Sinclair and possessed curves to set a man on fire deserved a husband who sought his pleasure other places than his own bed.

Her response to him was a sight to see. And certainly feel. He moved his head and slid his tongue into her mouth. The fact that she seemed startled confused him. However, it didn't take her long to join him. As much as he wanted to see where this would lead them, it was time to pack up and go.

He drew back and gave her a quick kiss on her nose. "I would love more than ye can imagine to continue this, but if we leave now we will make it to Castle Leod tomorrow, which means only one more night on the road and then we have the safety of the Mackenzies."

She stretched and he groaned. She grinned at him. "Ye snore."

"So do ye," he snapped back.

"I doona snore," she huffed.

She climbed out of bed, her skirts wrapped around her slim silky legs all the way up her thighs. He groaned again.

Megan shook out her hair and after finger combing it, quickly braided it and walked to the bowl of water on the table near the door and washed her face.

He was so mesmerized by all that she did, he forgot to get moving himself. Shaking his head, he climbed out of bed, drew on his boots and began to load up his dirks, swords, and satchel.

"I will wait outside the door while ye do what ye need to do. Once we are downstairs and the innkeeper is up and about, I will leave ye with him so I can take care of myself." With those words he left the room before he did what he wanted to do and toss her on the bed to finish what they'd just started.

MEGAN NODDED AS Gregory pulled the door shut. She closed her eyes and let out the breath she'd been holding. If he hadn't stopped, *she* would have had a problem stopping.

She remembered she and Robert had had some nice times when they were first married, but he shortly lost interest, and aside from his duty to her, he spent a goodly amount of time in other women's beds.

When she arrived downstairs, the strumpet from the night before was practically sitting on Gregory's lap. Thankfully, he did not look happy.

Megan took a seat at the table where Gregory was. She looked up at the server and said, "'Tis too bad, lass, that ye have to throw yerself at men to get attention. My husband and I had a quite a few laughs last night about yer pushy behavior."

She had hit the mark, which she was sure would happen. The lass did not like being laughed at. She immediately left them and stomped back to the kitchen.

Gregory leaned over and give her a quick kiss. "Thank ye, lass. I was getting close to shoving her off my lap, but didn't want to bring that much notice to myself. Let us eat and be on our way."

The innkeeper brought them bowls of porridge, warm bread and butter, along with two mugs of ale. He said nothing, but nodded at them. As he moved to return to the kitchen, he said, "Are ye leaving then, lad?"

"Aye," Gregory said. "We will be on our way when we finish our meal. I will settle our bill up with ye before we go."

The food was good and filling. Megan was ready to continue their trip. She was anxious to sleep in a real bed and warm herself in front of a fire.

Gregory grabbed her hand and with his other hand, picked up her satchel and a sack. "I asked the inn's cook to pack us food again, so we won't have to make many stops."

They walked to the stables and she ran her hands up and down her arms. "When will we meet up with the other men in your group?"

"Actually, it should be soon. We've been lucky so far, and I will feel better once there are six more of us."

The weather being cold with the sky covered with clouds, Gregory gave her the plaid that she wrapped around herself. They mounted their horses and left.

They rode in silence for a while, then Megan asked, "Why is it ye ne'er married?"

Gregory shrugged. "With my parent's marriage being not the best example and my da a difficult mon who dinna care how much he hurt my mam's feelings, I thought I would avoid all that."

Megan frowned. "Why would ye think ye would be the same?"

He hesitated. "There was a lass who I grew fond of, but before we were able to make any promises to each other she died from an ague. That's when I decided Fate was reminding me that marriage was no' in my future."

"Yet here ye are telling people at the inn that we are married, and unless ye've changed yer mind, ye still plan to do yer duty to me."

"Stop!" He pulled on his horse's reins and twisted her so they faced each other.

She stared at him wide-eyed. He rested his hands on her shoulders and looked into those eyes. "Aye, maybe when I left Castle Leod to fetch ye I was doing my duty, but that is no' why I plan to marry ye now." With those words, he pulled her close to his body and took her mouth in a kiss of passion like she'd never felt before.

Megan jolted as something hard hit her in her upper arm. She felt herself begin to slump in Gregory's arms and then everything went black.

⟫⟪

GREGORY'S WARRIOR ROLE went into immediate action. He gently laid Megon on the ground, straddled her and withdrew his bow from his shoulder. He loaded an arrow, looking around.

A loud whooping came from the direction behind him. He turned and prepared to shoot, then stopped as he recognized the Mackenzie warriors arriving from the north.

The men noticed Megan on the ground, bleeding, and silence followed their arrival. Expecting an attack, Gregory withdrew his sword as did his men while they slid from their horses. They formed a circle around Megan, their backs to each other.

The only sounds were those of small animals scurrying

around. "Who the devil was that?" Francis asked, breathing hard, still holding his sword at the ready.

"I doona ken." He waved at the men. "Four of ye circle the area and see what ye can find. The other two stay with us." He turned his attention to Megan. An arrow stuck out of her upper arm. "I'm sorry, darlin' but this is going to hurt." Even though she was still passed out, he felt the need to reassure her.

He broke the end of the arrow off, leaving the rest of it in her flesh. If he pulled it out, she could bleed to death. "We have to get her somewhere we can get help. We're no' close enough to home."

"We're at the end of Ross land. We have an alliance with them. We can bring Lady Sinclair to Balnagown," Alexander said.

Gregory nodded and the two who remained with him and Megan moved to their horses.

"One we arrive at Balnagown, ye two come back here and help the others find our attackers. Because nothing has happened since Megan was shot, I doona think it's Gunn's men. Unless this was the one who has been tracking us."

Gregory lifted Megan into his arms and swung his leg over the horse. With the other two men surrounding them, he headed to Balnagown Castle.

CHAPTER TWELVE

MEGAN AWOKE WITH a dreadful pain in her arm. She looked around the room she was in and didn't recognize it. What happened? The last she remembered she and Gregory were on his horse and then he... Where was Gregory?

"Right here, lass."

She turned to her right side and black dots appeared in her eyes and her arm screamed with pain.

"Easy, Megan. Doona move too much. We're waiting for the healer to come."

She took a few deep breaths to help calm herself. "What happened?"

"Ye were shot with an arrow in yer arm." The look on his face was almost as painful as her arm.

Almost.

Megan closed her eyes. "The Gunn found us, then?"

"I doona think so, but I have my men out searching the area where ye were shot."

She looked up at him where he sat alongside her on the bed. "Did we make it all the way to Castle Leod?"

Just then the door to the bedchamber opened and a woman of middle years hustled into the room, a basket over her arm. She had a cheerful way about her, a plump body and a big smile. "I am Mrs. Bridget Ross, the clan healer." She moved over to the bed and looked at Megan with sympathy. "Are ye the poor lass who was shot?"

"Aye," Gregory said.

Megan did not recognize the healer, but she thought Gregory had referred to the one at Castle Leod as Emma. While the woman searched through her basket, Megan looked over at Gregory. "Where are we?"

"Balnagown Castle. Ross lands."

Her hopes that the dreadful trip was over were dashed. "Are we far from Castle Leod?"

"Not really. Normally a full day's ride, but with yer injury we must take it slow. Most likely a day and half if we're in luck."

Mrs. Ross stepped up to the bed. "Sir, ye must leave now as I must undress the lass and take the arrow out."

Megan reached out. "Nay! Gregory is my husband. I need him to stay."

The woman glanced briefly at Megan's hand, the one missing a wedding ring and shrugged. "If that is yer wish, lass, then that is fine with me."

Megan let out a sigh of relief. The thought of Gregory leaving her while enduring whatever it was the healer had to do terrified her. She was in a strange place with a very painful injury.

Suddenly feeling very sorry for herself, tears filled her eyes. She turned her head the other way so Gregory wouldn't see her fall apart.

As the woman undressed her, she thought about how her life, though not the wonderful one it could be had been, had been ripped out from under her. Anthony had tried to force her to marry The Gunn, then when she climbed out the window, she was lucky she didn't break her neck after which followed the race to avoid their pursuers.

And now this.

Despite her best efforts to hide her distress, Gregory kicked off his boots and climbed on the bed beside her non-injured side. Since they'd told the healer that they were married, she didn't worry about what the woman thought.

He gently put his arm around on her shoulder, avoiding the arm the healer had started working on. "'Tis all right, sweeting, Ye can let go."

That was all she needed to release all the pain, fear, and fatigue she'd suffered since Robert's death. The tears would just not stop. Gregory rubbed her back and held her as she screamed when the healer pulled the arrow from her arm.

Another woman walked into the room. "Bridget. do ye need help?"

"Aye, I need ye to press the cloth over her injury while I sew her up."

Megan rested her head on Gregory's chest. It amazed her how comforting it was to have him hold her. She smiled, thinking how they keep telling people they were married and wondered that when Anthony caught up to them, if he would agree.

She closed her eyes and winced as the needle went in and out of her arm. "I think I'm going to empty my stomach."

"Do ye think ye can hold out for a few more minutes? If not, I'll get ye a chamber pot."

GREGORY HAD BEEN sewed up a few times himself and hated that the woman under his care had been injured. He'd been so fascinated by Megan and distracted by the attraction he felt for her that he forgot himself and the fact that they were being tracked.

Once she was well enough to travel, they would head to Castle Leod as quickly as her bruised body could make it. She would never be allowed to leave the keep unless he had a guard with her.

As she twitched and tears ran down her face, he wished he'd thought about asking the healer for some whisky for her.

And for him too.

It seemed like forever, but finally the healer said, "I'm finished, lass. Ye can relax now."

Megan closed her eyes and nodded. "Thank ye." Her voice came out in a weak whisper.

Gregory meant to stand, but Megan grabbed his hand and sobbed. "Nay, doona leave me."

He watched the healer as she began to pack up. "Is there something ye can give the lass for the pain?"

"I can have a tisane mixed for her. It will also help her to sleep, which is the body's best way to heal itself."

He looked down at her. "How is yer stomach, Megan?"

She wiped her eyes and looked up at him with such a pitiful expression on her face that he wanted to find the mon who'd shot her and run his sword through him.

"I feel a bit more settled."

"I'm sure with the way I acted crossing the mountain pass and now falling apart on ye, ye must think me the silliest lass ye ever met."

"Nay. Ye've been through a lot. Ye are a verra brave lass, and I'm anxious to get ye safely to Castle Leod so ye can rest and settle in."

The bedchamber opened and a young lass entered. "The laird asks that I see if ye want food sent up here or will ye be joining them in the great hall."

Gregory shook his head. "Nay, my wife is feeling quite unsettled, so if ye can bring food up for me and maybe some tea or broth for her that would be greatly appreciated."

Before she left another lass appeared with a mug and approached Megan. "This is the tisane the healer sent up for ye."

Gregory took the mug from the maid. "Thank ye. I will see that she drinks it, but I want her to have something in her stomach first."

Both lasses left and Gregory smoothed the hair back from Megan's forehead. Her eyes were closed so he took the time to study her face. The pain, fatigue and fear she'd suffered since Robert's death was clearly on her face. But she was still a beautiful woman and he felt no regret on informing everyone that she was his wife.

Something he had never thought he would have and although he'd arrived at Sinclair Castle Girnigoe with the full intention of doing his duty by marrying Robert's widow, he had to admit to himself that he no longer felt as though having Megan Sinclair—now Mackenzie according to what they were telling everyone within hearing distance—for a wife was a duty.

He didn't know where this marriage would go, since he was sure Megan still thought he only planned to marry her as a duty.

Again the bedchamber door opened and Lady Ross entered carrying a tray.

"My lady, ye dinna have to bring the food yerself," Gregory said as he jumped from the bed to take the food from her.

She shook her head. "'Tis no problem, and I thought I should check and see how yer wife is doing." Lady Ross looked down at Megan, who still had her eyes closed, and was at this point hopefully asleep.

"I understand there is quite a story behind yer arrival. I ken ye spoke briefly to my husband when ye first appeared with the lass in yer arms."

Gregory set the tray down. "Aye. Once I get Megan to drink her tea and broth, I'll give her the tisane yer healer sent. Hopefully I will be able to spend whatever time ye and the laird can spare for me to tell ye what has happened. 'Tis my hope we have no' been followed, but ye ken to be aware of a possible danger."

Lady Ross smiled at him. "Ye just take care of the lass, and when ye have a moment we will both be happy to speak with ye."

With those words she took another look at a sleeping Megan and left the room.

He waited about fifteen minutes and then woke her up. "Here lass, ye need to take some broth, at least, and the tisane."

She went to move and winced and cried out, apparently forgetting her injury. Gregory put his hand on her back and helped her up.

He hoped they hadn't led trouble to the castle with their escape here.

CHAPTER THIRTEEN

A FTER A FEW days Megan was anxious to leave Balnagown and travel to her new home. Gregory had been so caring while she was recovering from her injury that she almost felt as though this marriage was possibly not just a duty to him.

Or perhaps this *was* just another duty. The whole thing had her tied in knots.

"Are ye ready, lass?" Gregory entered the bedchamber she'd been staying in just as she finished dressing. It was still painful, but she was determined to prove to herself that she was stronger than the weak lass that Gregory must think her to be, although he had assured her many times that she was not a weak, but a strong woman.

Why she wanted to appear strong to him was confusing. As were her feelings about the man. Once they arrived at his home she would certainly see the real man, not the one who rescued her and was so kind and caring.

And did his duty.

Gregory offered to carry her down the stairs, but she refused. "I can walk. I doona want ye treating me like a bairn."

He just smiled at her, almost as if she did sound like a bairn, which she did to her own ears.

She allowed him to put his arm around her shoulders, avoiding her sore arm as they made it down the stairs. "What if The

Gunn and his men are waiting for us?"

"Nay. I told one of the men with us that I sent to look for whoever shot ye to continue on to Castle Leod and ask Laird Mackenzie to send out men to meet us for the trip from here."

She frowned. "I am causing a lot of people much trouble."

"Ye are my wife."

Not able to help herself, she smirked. "Aye, ye did yer—"

Before she could continue, Gregory turned her and captured her mouth with his, carefully pulling her next to him.

She melted, forgetting how powerful this man's kisses were. Before she was able to settle in and really enjoy it, he released her and looked into her eyes. "Every time ye attempt to say that word, I will kiss ye."

Not thinking that was such a bad thing, mayhap she would throw that word out once in a while.

The men from Castle Leod had arrived and were settled in the great hall at a few tables, eating, when Gregory and Megan entered the room.

"So this is the wife that's caused so much trouble?" one of the men said as he grinned.

Gregory walked up to him and slapped him on the back of the head. "Doona let me hear ye say that again, or ye will be working in the kitchens for the next month." He turned to the rest of the men, and pointed at them. "That goes for all of ye."

Although he meant well, Megan was mortified. That was exactly what she'd been thinking.

Another of the men stood. "Mrs. Mackenzie, may I offer my apologies for the ignorant mon in our group." He bowed. "We all welcome ye to our clan and our castle—when we get there."

His smile made her smile back.

She wondered if they knew her marriage to Gregory had been an improper Scottish wedding. Would they still accept her?

"Lass, stop fretting." Gregory took her uninjured arm and moved her to the dais where Laird and Lady Ross sat. She'd had a few ladies' afternoons with the lady of the manor and a few of the other women in the keep as they did their mending. Lady Ross, who had told her to call her Marion, was a gracious and caring woman.

Unable to do any sewing due to her injury, she was happy just to be with women for a couple of hours each day after being with just men while they traveled.

Gregory brought Megan forward in front of his men. "I will introduce to all of ye my wife, Megan Mackenzie. Yer job will be to protect her from here to Castle Leod. As I ken ye have all been told, there are Gunn men and Sinclair men after her."

The men nodded as he spoke. "As any other member of the Mackenzie clan, I expect yer total dedication to her safety."

After a second of silence, a cheer erupted from the men.

Tears came to Megan's eyes again. If she didn't get to Castle Leod and settled in she would spend more time weeping.

After a breakfast of porridge, a boiled egg and a Bannock dripping with butter and honey, she felt revived.

Gregory smiled at her. "'Tis good to see ye eating. 'Twill help with yer healing."

She hated how her feelings were changing toward this man. This husband. He'd been very caring and sweet—how he would hate that term—but she still couldn't help but wonder what would happen when they arrived at Castle Leod and they both took up their daily lives.

Would she never see him? Would he be off on assignments for the laird? Would she be accepted by the clan? Would she have something useful to do with her time?

Another concern was the fact that even though they had this "marriage" it could be easy for Gunn to protest it since it was not done completely legally.

Then there was the matter of consummation. So far, everything Gregory had done in that direction had been very interesting and exciting.

And frightening.

She really didn't want to fall in love with this man, her husband. Not until she was convinced he cared for her that way. She sighed. So many things to worry herself over.

"If ye're finished, Megan, 'tis time we started. I want to ride as far today as we can. But, please be aware I doona want ye to ride longer than yer body can take. Because I think it will be easier on yer body, ye will ride with me again."

One thing she continued to notice was Gregory's tendency to order her about and decide what was best for her as if she wasn't adult enough to make her own decisions.

Since Robert was exactly the opposite, letting her do whatever she wanted, she wasn't quite sure what to make of this husband of hers.

Time would tell. All she wanted now was to make it to a permanent place with safety, no unexpected arrows, regular meals and a warm bed to sleep in. With her husband next to her?

GREGORY HAD NOT planned to feel more than an obligation to Megan and possibly friendship, and in the future, maybe affection.

However, things did not turn out that way. The more time he spent with her, and the more he took care of her, and the more he enjoyed her company, the more he was afraid what he hadn't planned on—falling in love—was happening to him.

So far he hadn't seen signs of his da in him. No matter how much Megan annoyed him—which she'd done little of except for her obsessions with his *duty*—it had never crossed his mind to raise his hand to her.

How could a grown man, a warrior as his da was, put his fists to a small, soft woman he had vowed before God to take care of? His conversation with Daniel came back. Just because his da was terrible to his mam didn't mean he would do the same.

Even though he knew it was not good for Megan to travel so hard, he pushed them all to travel without long breaks. He and his men had ridden before without stopping to sleep, and he made sure Megan was bundled up against him as many hours as she wanted to sleep. He was hoping the tisane the healer had given her before they left would help to make the trip easier on her sore body.

They brought food with them from Balnagown, along with fresh bandages so on their short stops he could make sure Megan ate and her bandage was changed.

Several men rode behind them, in front, and right alongside them.

There had been no reports of men following so either they had decided not to pursue them—which he didn't believe—or the Gunn was not as adept at travel as the Mackenzies were.

He breathed a sigh of relief when Castle Leod came into view. Never had he been so happy to see a place in all the times he'd been away on various assignments for Daniel.

He shook a sleeping Megan. "Megan, we're home."

She sat up, looking at the castle. "Home."

"Aye." All he wanted to do was take a dip in the loch to clean off all the road dust, have a decent meal and take his wife to bed. Hopefully her injury was healed at least as much as needed to take care of the swollen man's part he'd been riding on for days. And the promising kisses they'd shared.

They rode over the drawbridge, the sound of the horses' hooves pounding on the wood music to his ears.

CHAPTER FOURTEEN

"**N**AY, YE WILL no' share a bedchamber until ye had a proper wedding!" Lady Beth Mackenzie stood glaring at Gregory, her hands fisted on her hips. They had just arrived and Megan looked like she was about to faint. He'd just asked Lady Mackenzie to assign a bed chamber to them and when she inquired when they had married, they looked at each other and Beth frowned. "I'll have the story, please."

Gregory told them how they had announced themselves as married for most of the journey, so they were considered married by the laws of Scotland.

"No' by my laws," she said. "I will be sending for a priest to marry ye officially." The look on her face did not bode well for them to consummate their marriage anytime soon.

He sighed. "Just make sure ye do it right away. We have men coming after us to drag Megan off to marry someone she doesna wish to marry."

"I will send for Father Matthew who should be here in a day or two." She glared at Gregory. "Until then we will have a comfortable room prepared for Megan and ye can use yer usual room."

Unhappy, but bending to the rules that the Lady of the Manor insisted on, he put his arm around Megan. "My wife is no' well, she's recovering from a wound in her arm. She needs to rest. Can she no' use my bedchamber until the other one is ready?"

Beth nodded. "I can see she is no' well." She moved toward her and placed her arm around Megan's shoulder. "I will send for Emma who will care for her, and aye, she can use yer bedchamber until the other one is ready." She pointed at him, with no nonsense on her face. "Ye, stay away from there."

"I must first get clean clothes so I might take a wash in the loch."

Beth nodded.

"I see ye're laying down rules again, Wife." Daniel had joined them and grinned at Beth.

Gregory put his hand on Megan's arm. "My Laird, may I present to ye *my wife*"—he glared in Beth's direction—"Megan Mackenzie."

"'Tis a pleasure, lass."

Megan looked as though she was ready to collapse. "I will have a bath sent up for ye and send for Emma to look at yer injury," Beth said.

Daniel slapped Gregory on his back. "As soon as ye get back from the loch, stop in my solar for a short meeting. There are things I want to speak with ye about."

Gregory nodded and headed for the stairs to his bed chamber to retrieve much-needed clean clothes. He made sure Megan was comfortable with Beth, but knowing the laird's wife, she would take very good care of the lass and make sure she felt welcomed.

It was definitely welcome to arrive at his bedchamber. His plans for bedding his new wife shattered, he could only hope that the priest would arrive soon. He congratulated himself on how well he'd refrained from seducing the lass thus far. But it was important he not introduce his wife to bed sport—which he had reason to believe was not something she'd had received a great deal of pleasure from—until the time was right. Perhaps Lady Beth had the right idea of it.

He rummaged around in the trunk at the foot of the bed and

retrieved new clothes.

Once he arrived at the loch behind the castle, he stripped down and dove into the cold water.

MEGAN AWOKE FROM her nap and looked around. So this was Gregory's bedchamber. She almost laughed at the expression on his face when Beth denied their marriage and insisted they sleep apart until their priest arrived.

She wasn't sure if she was happy or sad. She had mixed feelings about Gregory. She still didn't know if she was here only for duty or if his feelings for her had changed.

Her feelings? She was not sure. Based on his kisses, she was sure him bedding her would be different than it had been with Robert. He was caring where Robert just let her be. That was one point in his favor since she'd seen in Gregory so far that he enjoyed directing her life. So far she'd allowed it because she was too tired and unsettled to dispute what he'd said.

She yawned just as one of the maids entered. "I am sorry to disturb ye, but Lady Mackenzie wanted to be sure ye're settled in and didn't need help undressing."

Megan smiled. "That was verra sweet of her, and please thank Lady Mackenzie for me, but my dress is easily removed."

"If ye need anything else, please have one of the men in the corridor send for Sarah. I am usually in the kitchen."

"Thank ye so much, Sarah."

Not long after Sarah left, a few strapping lads carried in a bath tub, along with several buckets of water. She sighed at the thought of being clean again.

Before she climbed into the tub, there was a hard knock on the door.

Startled, Megan called, "Who is there?"

"'Tis me, Megan," Gregory said. "Open the door."

She moved closer to the door. "Nay. I am ready to take my bath."

"I need to check yer injury."

"Emma has already looked at it. She said it looked as though it is healing well."

Silence for a few minutes, so Megan assumed Gregory was gone, and put her foot into the water.

"Be sure to keep yer injury out of the water."

Megan huffed. "Gregory. I doona need ye telling me what to do all the time, or telling everyone else what they need to do for me. I am a grown woman and I can make decisions for myself. Right now, I intend to enjoy my bath. So please leave me be."

He mumbled something she couldn't hear followed by the sound of his boots as he walked away.

With a sigh, she climbed into the tub and settled herself, careful to leave her bandage out of the water, something she would have done anyway, even if the arrogant oaf hadn't ordered her to do it. She huffed.

Two days had passed since Megan and Gregory had reached the Castle Leod. Father Matthew had arrived the night before and the wedding and celebration following the event had finally arrived. Poor Beth had been racing around the keep, meeting with the cook and seeing to all matters having to do with the celebration.

If Megan had any reservations about getting on with Beth, they had vanished. She found Beth very easy to deal with. After hearing about the sisters Beth was raised with, she understood. Never having had a sister, she found it very pleasant to have another woman to share chores with and time in the solar in the afternoon while they sewed, embroidered and chatted.

Gregory had not been in the best of moods when he saw her as they met during the day in the keep and at the meals they'd shared with the family in the great hall. He continued to grumble about Beth's declaration that he could not enter his own bed chamber.

Megan was suffering from nervous jitters. Even more so than when she married Robert. Then she had no idea what to expect and was, if she was honest, later disappointed. She'd heard some of the maids speaking about activities in the marriage bed and she knew she was not feeling what they had.

Many times she'd considered asking Beth about the marriage bed, then felt silly since she'd been married for almost two years.

The only thing she knew for sure was that it was hard, being barren.

After a soft knock, the door to the bedchamber opened and Beth—literally—danced into the room. "My dear, 'tis time to get ye dressed for yer wedding."

A few other women followed, one carrying a beautiful gown, another the Mackenzie plaid which would be draped over her shoulder and anchored with a brooch to show her acceptance of the Mackenzie clan.

Since she'd already had her bath, the women began to dress her, and then one of them started on her hair, weaving ribbons throughout her tresses. When she stood in front of the looking glass she was stunned.

She was pretty!

Did Gregory think so?

She brushed off the silly thought and picked up the flowers someone had found for her and had fixed into a small bouquet. Placing her hand on her fluttering stomach, she looked at the women grinning at her. "I'm ready."

It was a short distance from the castle to the kirk. She and Beth walked with the other women who chatted excitedly. The air was clean and fresh, a typical Highland day with signs of winter's approach.

Questions filled her mind as they drew closer to the wedding site. Would this marriage make her happy? Had she made a mistake in agreeing to a vow that was made when her husband was merely no more than a lad?

Would Gregory grow to resent her because any choice he might have had for a wife was taken from him?

Megan smiled at Apex who shook his head at her, seeming to stand guard as they arrived at the kirk. Then Beth took her hands in her ice-cold ones and squeezed. "I can hear yer thoughts as we walked. I ken Gregory verra well. He is good, honorable mon and will do all that is necessary to make ye happy."

Feeling somewhat eased by Beth's words, Megan entered the kirk where she looked up the aisle at Laird Daniel Mackenzie and Father Matthew, and then to Gregory. After that, she had eyes for no one else.

The man was stunning.

She'd seen him every day for some time, but now, standing there dressed in his formal Mackenzie attire, his wavy black hair pulled back, and with shorter hair falling onto his forehead as he stood and spoke with the laird, she could not take her gaze off him.

After a few words from Daniel, Gregory turned and looked at her with those deep blue eyes and she almost stumbled. Most likely knowing her thoughts, he grinned.

And she blushed.

This was it.

Whether Gregory was marrying her for duty or any other reason, there was no turning back now. She had every reason to believe Gunn and Anthony were still after her. Robert's uncle had been too quick and too insistent to see her re-married to allow her to run off.

She arrived next to Gregory and he took her hands in his. "Lass, ye look beautiful, but yer hands are freezing." He shook them a bit and smiled at her. "Relax. This is only the formal profession of what we've been saying in public for a couple of weeks now."

She leaned in and he bent toward her, so they were almost

nose to nose. "But this is real."

He grinned. "I ken. 'Tis what I've been waiting for." He had the nerve to wink and she was forced to grin back.

Father Matthew cleared his throat which told them he was ready to begin the service.

The priest raised their hands and placed them palm to palm. Then he took a piece of a Mackenzie plaid and wrapped it around their hands, tying the pieces together, performing the well-known "tying of the knot".

She'd heard the words before at her own wedding, but it seemed so different when the priest said them this time:

"Repeat after me. *I, Gregory James Mackenzie of Clan Mackenzie, take thee Megan Maria Sinclair to be my wedded wife, to have and to hold from this day forward, for better for worse, for richer, for poorer, for fairer or fouler, in sickness and in health, to love and to cherish, till death us do part, according to God's holy ordinance and thereunto I plight thee my troth.*"

Gregory spoke his vows in a firm, clear voice and then she followed the priest to repeat her own vows in a shaky voice. Father Matthew gave them his blessings and then the official part of the ceremony was over. Gregory took Megan's face in his hands and kissed her much more enthusiastically than she thought the Church allowed.

When he pulled away, he winked at her and took her arm in his, tucking her alongside his large, warm body. Together they walked down the aisle away from the altar and outside to where Apex stood. Gregory lifted her into the saddle and climbed up behind her. They rode the short distance from the kirk to the castle, villagers trailing behind them, laughing and cheering.

She remembered when she and Robert had married with all the fuss like they were experiencing now. She 'twas a very excited young lass that day. Today, she was reluctant to expect too much.

In a short time, they'd ridden through the gates. Gregory helped her off the horse by lifting her with his hands wrapped around her waist. He slid her body down his and frowned. "Ye look concerned, lass. What troubles ye?"

She took his arm and shook her head. "Nothing." She smiled up at him, but it was apparent from his look that he did not believe her.

Did he know her so well already? Was that good or bad?

They made their way into the keep, hand in hand. The great hall had been decorated so beautifully considering how little time they had to do it. When Megan and Gregory sat at the head table, the villagers who had known Gregory for years took the opportunity to approach and wish him well. But Megan felt like they were focused on her with judgement. Did they find her wanting? Why was she so unsure of herself?

Once they were settled on the dais, the maids started bringing out platters of food, mostly breakfast items since the service was held in the morning.

Megan was a tad uncomfortable with how some of the maids eyed Gregory. Having been a single man for years she was certain many of the lasses glancing in his direction had warmed his bed many times.

She sighed. Hopefully her husband would not find her wanting, but she feared he would.

No man wanted a barren wife.

CHAPTER FIFTEEN

MEGAN DID ENJOY the party and she was happy during the wedding feast. The food was delicious and she always enjoyed dancing. Robert never cared for it, and usually sat with his friends and drank while she danced with whoever asked her.

On the other hand, despite his size, Gregory was a wonderful dancer and was on the dance floor longer than he was off. She tried to ignore all the lasses who came up to him to dance, with their hands extended.

Some of the men took her to the dance floor, but she would have preferred dancing with her new husband. Not that Gregory ignored her as Robert had, it just was that she was uncomfortable with the look on the lasses faces.

Was she jealous?

Definitely not. One had to be in love to feel jealous and she would not allow that. The last thing she needed was to be in love with a man who married her to fulfill a promise made years ago.

Isn't it about time to put that aside?

She would wait to make a decision on that until after the bedding. Then the disappointment on his face would convince her.

Megan sat at the table on the dais, recovering from her last dance. She looked up and Gregory was swaggering toward her, a soft smile on his face and a glint in his eyes. She swallowed several times, knowing exactly what he was planning.

He held his hand out. "Time for us to retire. We best do it before that bunch of drunken men at the table behind me decide to do a bedding ceremony."

She jumped up, remembering that with her first wedding. It was humiliating and Robert had thought it funny when the bedcover was whipped off her for him to get into the bed and dozens of men had whistled and commented on her naked body.

"We will make our way through the crowd separately, and then meet upstairs in my bedchamber. I doona think anyone will guess what we're doing until it's too late."

She nodded and Gregory turned and sat at the table with his friends. Megan slowly moved through the crowd, accepting wishes, and turning down dances.

Once she reached the stairs, she didn't look around, but just rushed upstairs. It took her a minute to remember which bedchamber was Gregory's. She sneaked open one door and knew she had found the right place.

Candles burned, and a jug of wine and two mugs sat on one table. The night shift she had wanted to wear was lying on the bed. Would Gregory be kind enough to let her wear it?

Since there were no women to give her a bath, she moved over to the table where she'd put her things when Beth and several others helped her move into Gregory's bedchamber.

She added one of her scented oils to the water in a bowl left for her and picked up one of the cloths to wash the sweat off her body from all the dancing.

Feeling refreshed, she slid into the night shift and moved over to the bed. She sat on the edge and within minutes the door opened and Gregory stood there.

Her heart began to pound and the sweat she'd so diligently wiped off came back again.

HIS BRIDE LOOKED scared to death. He found that surprising since she'd been married before. Certainly she knew what was going to happen?

He pulled on a pair of breeches under his kilt, then unwrapped the garment, leaving him in only the breeches and a léine. He looked over at her, sitting on the edge of the bed looking like she was about to bolt. He put his hand out. "Come join me for a cup of wine."

She took his hand with her ice-cold one. He led her to a chair in front of the brazier and took the chair alongside her. He poured them both a mug of wine, handed it to her and said, "So did ye enjoy yer wedding celebration?"

"Aye." She took a gulp of wine. "I enjoy dancing."

"So I noticed. I always enjoyed it myself."

Another gulp of wine. "It seems a lot of lasses enjoyed dancing with ye."

He grinned, even though she looked as though she was very sorry she'd said that. Taking pity on the lass he said, "Aye, just about the entire clan likes to dance."

She nodded. Another gulp. She held the mug out. "Can I have some more?"

He was starting to get nervous. Was she trying to get herself drunk? The last thing he wanted to do was bed a drunk wife. He poured about half a mug. "I think that is enough, lass."

She sighed. "Verra well." She did take her time sipping on that one.

Thinking the bed was making her nervous, he stood and lifted her up, then settled back in his chair and placed her on his lap.

She giggled.

Grinning himself, he took the mug from her hand and placed on it the table next to him. Taking her face in his hands he lowered his head. Just as he'd remembered. Soft, warm and plump lips. He slid his tongue along her lips and after a few moments she opened her mouth and he swept in.

He could have sworn she gagged, which he smiled at, but

eventually she seemed to settle in, and even touched his tongue lightly with her own.

Slowly, he slid the night rail off her shoulders, the garment pooling in her lap, revealing the most beautiful breasts he'd ever seen. Plump and firm with dark pink nipples begging to be touched. He ran his hands over her flesh, lightly running circles over her nipples with his palms. "Ye are so beautiful, Megan."

She looked at him. "Robert never—"

Gregory put his finger to her lips. "There are two people in this room, *mo chridhe*. Ye and me. No one else. Nor will there ever be."

He scooped her up and carried her to the bed while taking her mouth in a searing kiss. One of possession and desire.

He gently laid her on the bed and stepped back. "Give me a minute." He then proceeded to remove his various weapons making a messy pile on the floor.

Megan sat studying him, her eyes growing larger as each weapon dropped to the floor. Then she gulped and looked at his face as he removed his clothes. It was hard to decide what her face said, but instead of wondering, he climbed back on the bed and placed his hands under her hips to whip the night rail off and toss it on the pile he'd just made.

He admired her stunning body, all curves and lushness. Then he put his arm around her shoulders and slid them both down, facing each other. Once more he cupped her chin and lowered his head.

This time she was the one who slid her tongue along his lips which brought him a smile. Their tongues wrestled, their bodies each other touching in places that made them both groan.

He lowered his head to take one of her breasts in his mouth and suckled hard, teasing her nipple with his teeth. She drew in a deep breath and groaned.

He grinned.

Slowly he moved his hand down her body to the place he was eager to touch.

Megan jumped a bit. He moved his mouth to her other breast and ran his finger along the slightly swollen lips at her center. Her slight dampness told him she needed more time to be prepared for him.

He moved his mouth to her head and began to whisper in her ear, in Gaelic, of her beauty, how much he desired her, and how anxious he was to be inside her.

Once more he took one of her breasts in his mouth and tugged on her nipple. Megan sucked in a breath. "Aye. That feels good."

After a few minutes of his ministrations, he noticed she was growing wetter, so his attentions were working. He moved his thumb to her stiffened flesh and began to rub in circles.

Megan sucked in a breath. "Oh, aye, Gregory. That feels wonderful. Doona stop."

"I have no intention of stopping, *mo chridhe*. Just relax and let me do the work for ye."

He returned to her breast, sucking, circling, teasing as Megan shifted and became restless. "I feel so odd. But wonderful, too."

She pressed against his rapidly moving fingers. "There is something missing, husband."

"Relax, wife."

Within a minute or two her head began to thrash back and forth as she started to moan and suck in breaths. "What is happening?"

Gregory squeezed her stiffened flesh and Megan wrapped her arms around his shoulders and let out with a moan that had him more than ready to move on.

As he separated her legs and climbed between them, she looked at him, fright in her eyes. "Please go easy or it will hurt."

"Nay, lass, 'twill no' hurt, it will only feel good. I promise. I told ye I would ne'er hurt ye."

She still cringed and tensed as he entered her and then pushed lightly until he was snug against her warmth. A lone tear slid down her cheek. Gregory wiped it. "Are ye all right, lass?"

She nodded, a smile breaking out on her face. "Aye. It dinna hurt."

He decided to have a conversation with her later about her actions and what she said, but now he'd waited too long to enjoy her body.

Because he'd been denied his husbandly rights much longer than he'd wanted, he didn't last long. In no time at all it seemed, he thrust hard against her and poured his seed into her body.

CHAPTER SIXTEEN

LONG AFTER MEGAN had snuggled up against him and fell into a deep sleep Gregory lay on his back, his hands behind his head, and thought about their recent lovemaking. Until he talked to Megan, he didn't want to make any judgement on what he had begun to believe by her actions and comments.

It had appeared to him that his wife, having been married for almost two years, had never experienced an orgasm. It was true that it had taken him longer to get her ready for him than most lasses, but it hadn't been impossible.

Was it that Robert did not have the patience to prepare his wife properly? Is that why she thought it would hurt? It was true that he hadn't seen much of the man over the years since they'd trained together, but it would never occur to him that a man who was so active with the lasses when he knew him would be so neglectful of his own wife.

It took some time, but eventually he fell asleep with the questions still on his mind.

MEGAN AWOKE WITH a smile on her face and for a moment didn't know why. Then she felt an arm, a very strong arm, covered with wiry hair, wrapped around her middle, pulling her snug to warm, muscled flesh.

Her husband.

She smiled again. Last night's bed activities were nothing like the ones she shared with Robert. When they were first married, he had been gentle, but after a couple of weeks he told her she was lacking something that other women had.

She'd tried to find out what she was missing, and after a few months of nothing changing, and bed activities still hurting, she'd worked up the nerve to speak with one of the kitchen lasses who seemed to enjoy the lads very much. She said that since Megan had not produced a bairn, she was probably barren which could prevent her from enjoying the marriage bed.

So, barren women did not enjoy the marriage bed, and whatever dislike she'd developed for the activity rested with her inability to conceive a bairn.

After her night with Gregory, she was very confused and if it was not such an embarrassing matter, she would ask him about it. Not having had a mam growing up, mayhap she would talk to the midwife here and see if she thought the same thing as the kitchen lass. She had been reluctant to speak with the midwife at Sinclair Castle Girnigoe because 'twas her husband's home and she felt uncomfortable speaking with her.

Emma, the Mackenzie clan healer, however, was young and easy to speak with. Maybe she would seek her out and see if she could explain why she had a problem with Robert, but not Gregory.

She became distracted by something soft and moist nibbling on her neck. She grinned and turned to face her husband. "What are ye doing?"

"Bed activity is sometimes better in the morning." He continued to nuzzle her and his hand lowered to her breast and squeezed. "Ach, lass, ye have such perfect breasts."

She closed her eyes as warm feelings swept through her. "That feels good."

"'Tis happy I am to hear that since I doona intend to stop."

And he didn't stop. His hand left her breast and ran over her back to her bottom where he squeezed. "And yer arse is perfect, too."

She could feel the heat rise from her middle to her face. In a moment of daring, she slowly slid her hand down to wrap it around his male part, which she was surprised to find already hard.

"Aye, *mo chridhe*, keep doing that, it feels good."

Happy that she could do something that made him feel good since he'd done so much for her the night before, she continued to squeeze and slide her hand up and down.

Shortly, he put his hand over hers. "Ye better stop now or I won't have time to get ye ready for me."

Confused by his words, she shifted as his fingers once again moved to her woman's part. "Aye. I like that."

"Good, because I intend to do this until ye scream my name as ye come apart in my arms."

Whatever that meant, she was happy when he did similar things to her that he'd done the night before. She could get used to such things.

⇶✦⇷

MEGAN'S NOSE LED her to the kitchen where the cook was busy removing loaves of bread from the oven.

The woman grinned at her as she wiped her hands on a kitchen cloth. "How is the new bride this morning?"

Her question had the heat rising again from Megan's middle to her face.

The woman continued to study her. "Such a bonnie lass. Yer Gregory must be quite pleased."

To remove the attention from herself, she said, "I ken we are late to break our fast, but is it possible to get some food for us?"

"Of course. I ken Gregory will be training in the lists all day so he needs food. I will send in some porridge, oatcakes and ale for the two of ye to the great hall."

"Thank ye," Megan said and returned to the great hall where Gregory was waiting for her.

He was sitting at one of the tables with Daniel, the Mackenzie laird. From the short time she'd been at Castle Leod, she'd heard the story of how Beth Mackenzie had been thrown into the dungeon by a woman who'd wanted Daniel to marry her daughter instead.

Meanwhile Daniel had been frantically looking for Beth and had the entire castle searching as well.

It sounded like a very scary experience, but Beth was a sweet woman who welcomed her. Megan was very grateful for the lovely wedding Beth put together for her and Gregory.

"Good morning, Megan," Daniel said. "I was just discussing yer husband's role now that he's a married man."

She was quite surprised by the laird's statement since Anthony would never speak with a woman about what he was planning.

Did the laird know it had been an understanding between her and Gregory that he was marrying her out of duty and once the deed was done, he would go his way and she would go hers? Had Gregory not told him?

She had definitely changed her mind since then, and the thought of Gregory riding off and being gone for weeks, or even months, brought a heavy feeling to her stomach.

Before Daniel spoke again, a lass from the kitchen walked up to them and placed food on the table for her and Gregory. As they ate, Daniel spoke.

"We have problems with our borders, which all clans have. Reivers are expected, but when it gets too out of hand, we have to send men there."

Megan nodded as she ate, struggling to keep her food down as she waited for Daniel to tell her Gregory would be leaving soon to take care of this border problem. She braced herself for the news.

"Gregory will remain here. At least for a while, so he can see ye settled in. I hate to separate newly married couples, so for now my other second-in-command, Evan Mackenzie, will lead the men to the border."

Tears immediately flooded her eyes. She blinked quickly so no one at the table would believe she was such a weak lass. She was shocked at the laird's words. He would allow changes in his assignments to give them time together?

Anthony would never allow such a thing.

EVEN THOUGH MEGAN seemed quite surprised by Daniel's words, he wasn't. His cousin was a kind, caring man, but would deny such a title even if held to sword at his neck.

Despite their initial agreement to marry and go their own way, he was reluctant to leave Megan. He glanced over at his wife when Daniel spoke and saw the tension on her face until the laird told her of his plans.

Then she seemed quite relieved and even grinned after blinking away her tears.

He wasn't sure what that meant, but since this was a new home for her, she was probably glad to have at least one person in the keep that she knew.

She knows Beth and Daniel.

He blew out a breath of annoyance. So then now she knew three people.

Beth turned to Megan. "I could use help here at the keep. 'Tis a big place and at the end of the day I never feel that I finished all my tasks."

Megan nodded and swallowed her food. "Aye, my lady, I would love to help ye."

Beth smiled and placed her hand over Megan's. "Nay, lass, no 'my lady,' please call me Beth."

"Aye. Thank ye, my lad…" Megan grinned.

Daniel turned to Gregory and stood. "When ye're finished with yer meal, join me in my solar. Evan is at the list already, but I will summon him to join us."

Beth nodded at them and hurried off in the direction of the kitchen after being summoned by a lass. As the laird strode off, Gregory pushed his plate away and looked at Megan. "Are ye happy to work with Beth? She is a verra nice lass."

His wife smiled. "Aye. She is a wonderful woman. I am only too happy to help her."

Gregory cupped her chin in his hand. "Are ye happy I'm staying, even though that goes against what we agreed on at the beginning?"

Megan nodded. "Aye. 'Twill be more comfortable until I can settle in."

The redness that crawled up her face told him that might not be the only reason, but he wouldn't embarrass her by suggesting that.

He stood and kissed her on the top of her head. "I am off to meet with the laird."

CHAPTER SEVENTEEN

GREGORY ENTERED DANIEL'S solar right before Evan. Once they were all settled in chairs, Daniel leaned forward and placed his forearms on his thighs. "Two important matters, men. I need our warriors in top shape. Evan, I still want ye to go to the border, and Daniel, I am expecting the Gunn and the Sinclair to arrive any day."

Gregory's brows rose. "Indeed? What makes ye think so?"

Daniel leaned back in his chair. "I've had a couple of men watching the trails from both Clyth Castle and Sinclair Castle Girnigoe. One of the men reported back early this morning that there is a large contingent of men with both the Sinclair and Gunn banners only a day or so from us."

Gregory let out a low whistle. "Do ye think they came to fight?"

Daniel shrugged. "I doona think so. My mon said there weren't enough to forge a battle, but enough to ken they had something important on their mind."

"My wife," Gregory said.

Daniel nodded. "Aye."

Evan glanced between Daniel and Gregory. "What is yer plan, laird?"

"I will see what they have to say. Why they would arrive without enough forces to wage a battle leads me to believe they have another method of taking Megan."

Gregory snorted. "Let them try. I doona care what they come with. I'm no' giving up Megan. She is my wife and will stay just that way."

Daniel nodded. "I agree. I have no intention of turning the lass over no matter what information or method they arrive with."

The laird slapped his legs and stood. "Just be sure our men are prepared for battle, even though I doubt there will be one." He turned to Evan. "I will postpone yer trip to the border until the Gunn and Sinclair have arrived and speak their piece."

Gregory left the solar more concerned than he had pretended in the meeting. The only way they would be able to take his wife was if they grabbed her when she was alone. Any other way would cause anyone who put their hands on her to lose their head.

As he headed to the list to work with the men, he thought about whether he should tell Megan or not. As an adult woman, she had the right to know, but he didn't want to worry the lass if whatever Gunn and Sinclair hoped to do would be only speak with them.

It didn't matter. No one was taking Megan from him. They were legally married by the church, so whatever nonsense The Sinclair thought he could get away with would never work. Otherwise, there would be a battle, even if he had to fight it by himself.

TWO DAYS LATER Megan entered the kitchen and came to an abrupt stop only to have what felt like a brick wall walk into her immediately. She turned to see one of the warriors behind her. "Is there something amiss, John?"

He shrugged with a guilty look on his face. "Nay. I was just going to see about getting a couple of oatcakes."

She watched him go to the table against the wall and pick up two oatcakes. He smiled at her and walked toward the great hall.

It was very odd to see one of the warriors in the keep during the time they were to be on the list. She'd noticed how during the last couple of days she seemed to be tripping over warriors all day.

Later, when the keep doors were opened and the vendors piled in to sell their wares, Gregory left the list and walked up to her asking if he could join her as she browsed. She just looked up at him and stared, then shrugged. Things were strange, indeed.

***

It was the evening meal and Daniel, Beth, Gregory, Evan, and she sat at the dais, waiting for the lasses to bring out the food. They were all busy with conversations when a man hurried into the great hall. "Laird, they are here."

Daniel, Gregory, and Evan all stood. Megan tugged on the cuff of Gregory's léine. "Who are here?"

"Yer uncle and The Gunn."

She jumped up as if to run away when Gregory grabbed her around the waist. "Doona go anywhere lass. Stay next to me no matter what anyone says."

All the days of being guarded when the men were pretending they were not guarding her finally made sense. They must have known that Anthony and The Gunn were on their way.

"Ye kenned about this, dinna ye?"

Gregory looked down at her with an expression that she didn't quite understand, but brought tingles to her stomach. "Aye, we did, but I dinna want ye to be worried about it."

She placed her hand at her hip and smirked. "That was the reason for all the men following me. And here I thought I had become so bonny that I was attracting men."

He wrapped his arms around her. "Ye doona need any other mon but me."

She patted his arm. "Aye."

Daniel motioned to Gregory and Evan. "We will meet them at the gate."

Megan grabbed onto Gregory's sleeve. "I am coming, too."

"Nay. Ye stay here."

"Why? Ye ken why they are here. I should be allowed to speak for myself."

"'Tis dangerous."

She continued to hold onto his sleeve as he walked, running to keep up with him. "'Twould ne'er be dangerous for me with ye alongside me."

Gregory came to an abrupt halt and looked down at her. "'Tis true, lass. I would ne'er let anyone hurt ye."

She flushed and instead of trying to get her to stay in the keep, he took her hand. They linked fingers and walked together to the gate.

Daniel was already there with Evan alongside him, talking with Anthony and The Gunn.

"There she is!" The Gunn pointed at her. "My intended wife. I shall take her with me now."

Gregory tensed and held onto Megan's hand a tad tighter. "Ye have wasted yer time, Gunn. Megan and I are married, so she canno' marry ye."

The man whipped out a piece of parchment from his pouch and waved it. "This is a direct order from the king. Lady Megan Sinclair is to marry me."

A bit taken aback by that news, he wrapped his arm around his wife as she whimpered.

Daniel stepped forward and reached out. "I would see that paper." He moved back to where Evan, Gregory, and Megan stood. He opened it up and read it, then handed it to Gregory.

It was an order from the king that Robert Sinclair's widow was to marry Laird Stephen Angus Gunn of the Gunn Clan immediately up receipt of this order and it was signed by King George II, with his seal upon the paper.

Gregory tossed it back to The Gunn. "'Tis no matter to me because Megan Mackenzie and I were married before a priest of the church a couple of weeks ago."

"There can be an annulment," The Gunn shouted.

Gregory grinned and looked down at Megan. "Nay, there is no reason for an annulment."

All the soldiers standing behind Daniel, Evan, Gregory, and Megan drew their swords.

"As stated, there are no grounds for an annulment, so I suggest ye take yer men and return home. Megan Makenzie is a member of the Mackenzie Clan now and as her laird I will not permit her to leave with the two of ye," Daniel said.

Gregory knew exactly what those words meant. Daniel had refused an order of the king and he must have known the two men trying to rip his wife from him would not let it go.

The two men now had the monarch behind them.

"I would offer ye food and drink, but considering what ye came here for, I doona trust ye in my keep." Daniel placed his hands on his hips and studied the men.

"'Tis an outrage!" The Gunn screamed. He waved the order toward Megan. "Ye canno' defy an order of the king."

The men behind the Mackenzie clan members, who still had their swords out, moved forward. Evan spoke. "My men will see ye out of the castle."

Even though the Gunn and Sinclair had men behind them, too, Sinclair turned and waved his men toward the gate. A wise decision since Daniel could empty out the men practicing on the list and slaughter the ones with Gunn and Sinclair in a matter of minutes.

Once they were gone, Megan turned to Gregory, her hands twisting. "What are we going to do? Will I have to marry The Gunn?"

Gregory took both of her hands in his. "Calm yerself, lass. No one will make ye marry anyone because ye are mine. He can bring the king right here and I will no' let ye go."

She burst into tears, and Gregory wrapped his arms around her. Daniel, Evan, and the other men left them and returned to the keep.

CHAPTER EIGHTEEN

DAYS WENT BY and they heard nothing from Anthony. After he'd left, Megan had been nervous, jumping at every sound behind her. Daniel assigned one of his warriors to stay with her all day. Gregory had forbidden her from leaving the castle, and she was not allowed to go to the vendors when they came unless she had no one but Gregory at her side.

Having all these restrictions made her more nervous because there was no way for her to forget that the king ordered her to marry The Gunn. If there was a way to have her marriage annulled, she was certain Anthony would find it, even though it had been blessed by the Church and duly consummated. He seemed almost desperate to have her marry The Gunn, and she would love to know what his reward was for this.

Today she was resting in Beth's solar with her. Beth was beginning to develop a little belly bump and she found it hard to make it through the day without a nap. Luckily, her appetite was now normal.

It was right after the nooning and they would go over the tasks in the keep and who would take care of which one. As Beth moved farther into her condition, with her fatigue and occasional stomach upset, Megan had been taking on more of the duties.

Beth laid down the embroidery she was working on and studied Megan for a minute. "Ye seem nervous, Megan. Ye surely ken that Gregory and Daniel willna let ye go."

Megan nodded. "Aye, but I feel as though I'm bringing trouble to yer clan."

"'Tis ye clan now, Megan Makenzie," Beth said softly.

She couldn't hold the tears that sprang to her eyes. Aye, she felt as if this was her home. Robert had left her alone so much that she never really felt as though she was accepted at Sinclair Castle.

Anthony had pushed her away once he took over the lairdship, and Robert had spent his time training on the list and visiting the pub with his friends. It had been a lonely life. The only time her husband had sought her out was when he wanted to attempt once more to get an heir from her. Always after lovemaking and the pain she endured as he entered her, he would remind her there was something wrong with her. She spent the day remembering how unhappy she'd been then, and realizing how happy she was now.

She went about her chores, not realizing she was smiling until one of the maids mentioned it to her.

A few hours later, "Raise the drawbridge," echoed through the outer bailey.

Megan and Beth jumped up. "That doesn't sound good," Beth said.

They both hurried from the solar and made their way downstairs.

It appeared Daniel and Gregory had called half the men from the lists inside, leaving the other half to guard the outside of the castle.

"DO THEY REALLY believe they can breach our castle?" Gregory asked Daniel.

"Come, let us go up to the ramparts and see what they've

brought with them."

The two men made their way upstairs. "What does it look like?" he asked one of the men on duty.

"A large group to be sure, laird, but nothing we canno' handle."

Gregory stepped up to the wall and looked down. "I doona see any of King George's men." For that, he was grateful since they would not be waging a battle with the monarch which could be verra bad for their clan.

"I have an idea, laird," Gregory said. "Once we dispatch these men, I will take Megan to the Mackays until this is o'er."

Daniel hesitated for a moment, then said, "Aye. 'Tis a good one. If the lass isna here, there would be no reason for their return once we send them on their way now."

Anthony, with The Gunn standing next to him, cupped his hands around his mouth and shouted, "We come in peace."

Daniel and Gregory looked at each other and laughed. "Indeed," Daniel called down to them. "If ye come in peace, why do ye have triple the men ye had with ye the last time ye tried to snatch Gregory's wife?"

The Gunn shouted, "Once ye send my betrothed down to me, we will be on our way."

Daniel sighed. "We doona have a betrothed of yers here. We have been over this before. If ye are referring to Megan Mackenzie, she is wife to my cousin and second-in-command, Gregory Mackenzie. Her home is here with the Mackenzie clan. 'Tis sorry I am for yer trouble, but ye can be on your way now."

The Gunn waved the parchment in his hand, his face as red as a summer rose. "I have an order signed by King George II."

Daniel rested his forearms on top of the battlement and grinned. "So ye have said. And we have a marriage certificate signed by a priest. I believe God outranks the king."

The Gunn grew even redder in the face and shook his fist. "Her uncle, Laird Anthony Sinclair, signed a legal betrothal agreement between him and me, agreed to by the king."

Daniel shrugged. "So marry Sinclair then."

The men behind him snorted.

"And," Daniel continued, "the last time I heard, the Church dinna allow a woman to marry two men."

The Gunn nudged Sinclair in the ribs. He mon looked up. "I am the lass's uncle and responsible for her. I demand ye send her down here."

"Ye are no' the lass's uncle. Ye are her deceased husband's uncle. The only mon responsible for Megan Mackenzie is her husband, Gregory Mackenzie."

Daniel turned to Gregory. "I grow weary and 'tis close to the time for the evening meal." He looked down at the two men. "We will discuss this no further. Be off with ye, or I will have my men escort ye off Mackenzie land." With those words, Daniel turned toward the door to the steps, with Gregory following him.

'Twas a few hours later when shouting and the sound of swords clashing drew the attention of the men sitting at the dais table, drinking mugs of ale.

Daniel, Gregory, and Evan jumped up, drawing their swords and raced towards the keep door. Daniel looked over his shoulder and spotted Megan and Beth. "Off with ye both. Go to Emma's room and help her prepare for injuries."

"What about the servants?" Beth asked.

"Send those who are too nervous to help to the basement."

MEGAN AND BETH hurried to Emma's bothy located in the corner of the keep, and found her pulling bandages and clean linens from her shelves. She turned to Megan. "Can ye crush these herbs?" She handed her a bundle of herbs wrapped in a cloth. "I had intended to do that today, but one of the clan member's lads fell from a tree and scraped up his leg and arm."

"'Tis all right, Emma, I've done this many times before."

Megan sat and started pounding the leaves into powder. The warm scent of the familiar herbs actually calmed her.

As time when on they could still hear the sounds of battle but they were all certain The Gunn and Sinclair would be dispatched in due time.

Beth and Emma moved around the space, wiping down the surfaces of the tables and counters. "The lad bled a bit on this table, and I doona want to have a dirty place to put an injured warrior."

The noise of the battle never grew, but after about a half hour a warrior was brought in from the Gunn clan. He was cranky and insisted on being released to have their own healer deal with him.

"Yer clan healer is nowhere near us," Emma said to the grouchy warrior. "I doona care if ye are a Gunn, Sinclair, or Makenzie. I am a healer and ye are here, with messed up legs, and I'm going to patch ye up."

She looked at his injury and shook her head. "I doona think ye will be leaving anytime soon, mon. What happened to ye?"

"No' yer business. Just send me back out to my clan."

She placed her hands on her hips and sighed, as if speaking with a young lad. "Ye canno' walk, or do ye no' remember being carried in? I certainly can't carry ye and I have no intention of going out to the battle and finding someone to move ye. And tell me, what good would ye do for the battle if ye can't even stand?" She bent over and got in his face. "Now will ye tell me what happened to yer legs?"

The warrior spewed out a stream of language that should not be used in front of a lass, but Megan knew pain could do that to a man. "One of the *Mackenzie* horses, whose rider could no' control, fell on my legs."

Emma seemed unmoved by the outburst, and said, "Once I examine ye I can let ye ken how soon ye would be able to leave. But," she held up her hand as he started to speak, "if ye doona follow my directions ye might be here until yer old age."

He snarled.

Emma shrugged and just went on with her work and began to gather the things she would need.

Things grew quiet and all three women looked up. "It sounds as if the battle is over."

"Let me up, so I can join my clan," the mon lying on the table said.

"Nay," Emma said.

"Do I need to fight my way out, lass?"

Emma bent over him and said, "I wouldna try that if I were ye."

"Why?" He growled.

"Because. Ye. Canno'. Walk."

Emma took a cloth and placed it over the mon's face. Within seconds he was out as if someone had hit him over the head.

"What was that?" Beth asked.

"My little secret," Emma said. She grinned. "'Tis a way to settle someone. I learned this from a healer who had spent time in Prussia, where it was first used to control spasms, but it tends to knock people out, too. Especially if they are no' used to it. But 'tis necessary to be verra careful with it, so I seldom use it, but this—" she motioned to the patient—"was a necessary occasion."

Just then a warrior entered the bothy. "I was sent by Gregory Mackenzie to escort Megan Mackenzie to where he is."

Megan stood and brushed off her hands. She looked at the warrior. "Is Lady Mackenzie also needed?"

"Nay. Yer husband only requested ye."

Megan left the room with him and followed along the back wall of the keep. "Where is he?"

"No' far, just a few more steps."

Just as she was about to turn back, someone grabbed her from behind and placed a heavy hand over her mouth and wrapped a solid arm around her middle. She was dragged, struggling all the way, to an opening in the castle wall she'd not seen before. A man on the other side of the gaping hole grabbed her by her chin and pulled her through after placing his other hand on her mouth and nose. She panicked, thinking she would suffocate, and began in earnest to attempt to release herself.

"Stop wiggling, or I will have to knock ye o'er the head, and The Gunn will no' be happy about that," the man on the other side groused. He held her close to his body, his arm of steel wrapped around her, his hand over her mouth.

The Gunn? Good Lord I'm being kidnapped!

CHAPTER NINETEEN

GREGORY AND DANIEL watched from the ramparts as the warriors from the Gunn and Sinclair clans retreated. From what they'd seen, there had been a few injuries on their sides, nothing on the Mackenzies. Daniel had allowed the injured to visit with Emma.

"That was verra strange," Daniel said, shaking his head.

Gregory nodded. "Aye. They dinna last verra long. Almost as if they expected to lose."

Daniel slapped Gregory's back. "Well, for whatever reason they're gone, as far as I know we had no injuries, and hopefully they are gone for good."

They went to the great hall where they ordered whatever food that was in the kitchen and ale. The servants were slowly returning to their duties since the battle was over.

One of the maids placed a platter of apples, cheese, bread and butter on the table in front of them. They enjoyed the limited feast and within minutes, it seemed, Evan returned from the battle.

"How did it go, Evan?" Daniel asked. "Based on what we saw, we dinna think it was necessary for myself and Daniel to join in the fray."

Evan settled himself on the bench and reached over to take some of the offerings on the platter. "It was, by far, the strangest attack on a castle I have ever seen, or heard of."

"'Twas obvious they had no chance of getting into the castle to grab Megan, so why did they even try?" Gregory asked.

"Well, since we still have a couple of hours until evening meal, I'm going to check with Emma and see about the injuries she's treating."

Gregory thought about going with Daniel to check on Megan, but knowing she was busy with Emma, he decided instead to join the men who had fought in the battle to get some ideas from them about how it went. He left the great hall and headed to the lists.

❊❊❊

MEGAN STRUGGLED AND at one point even bit the hand of the man who was keeping her mouth covered. "Stop lass, or I will cause ye some injuries. 'Twill be easy for me to convince The Gunn that ye injured yerself."

Tired from the struggle, anyway, Megan stopped wiggling and took a deep breath. The man who'd originally grabbed her trotted over to two horses standing quietly near a large tree. He jumped up on one of the horses and reached down for Megan.

The other man released her and she opened her mouth to scream, but was immediately silenced by a smack on the back of her head.

❊❊❊

SHE HAD NO idea how long she'd been out, but the jostling of her body on the horse made the pain in her head excruciating. Her mouth was now free, but she knew she was far enough from the castle that she could scream her head off—which would hurt her head even more—and no one would hear her.

"Why are ye doing this?" she asked, softly. Even that caused the pain to radiate through her skull.

"'Tis none of yer business, lass. We were sent by The Gunn and The Sinclair to bring ye to them."

"If ye are bringing me to the devils, 'tis certainly my business." Not wishing to increase her pain, she remained silent for the remainder of the trip, which lasted less time than she'd expected.

The sound of men talking awoke her from a deep sleep. Her head didn't hurt quite as much, but still hurt like the devil.

Anthony and The Gunn walked up to where her rider came to a stop. "Well, look who's here," Anthony said. "My favorite niece and yer betrothed."

"I am no' yer niece and I am not his betrothed."

Anthony lips tightened. "Aye, ye are and we are headed to Edinburgh to have yer fake marriage to Gregory Mackenize annulled."

"Ye are no' making sense. I hope ye're no' planning on using that pretend order from the king. Ye ken Gregory—*my husband*—and I have a marriage certificate signed by the priest who performed the ceremony. If ye plan to petition the king for an annulment, ye will be breaking the laws of the church."

Anthony looked at The Gunn and they both smirked. "Well, I guess ye will have to wait until we arrive in Edinburgh."

She didn't like the sound of that.

GREGORY SAT AT the dais with Daniel and Beth awaiting the evening meal. His visits with the various warriors who had chased off The Gunn and The Sinclair came up with no other information that would help to explain what the men had been trying to do.

"Emma must have been busier than I thought," Gregory said. "I dinna realize the Gunn men had so many injuries."

Just then Emma walked down the steps from the first floor and headed toward the kitchen.

Gregory frowned at seeing Emma, since he assumed she was with Megan. He stood and walked through the great hall and caught up with her in the kitchen. "Did ye leave Megan to watch the injured?"

Emma looked up at him, confusion on her face. "Megan left me a few hours ago."

Gregory's stomach muscles tightened. "What do ye mean? I thought she was with ye helping out?"

"Aye, she was, but she left when ye sent the warrior to bring her to ye."

He frowned. "I dinna ken what ye mean. I dinna send anyone for her. Who was this warrior?"

Emma shrugged. "I doona ken. There are so many warriors. I doona ken them all."

"What did this warrior say?"

"He approached Megan and said ye wanted him to bring her where ye were."

His heart began to pound. "How long ago was this?"

Beginning look very nervous, Emma said, "Right after the Gunn and the Sinclair left."

Oh no. Gregory turned on his heel and strode back to the great hall. He stepped up to Daniel. "They took her."

Daniel jumped up, spilling his ale all over the table. There was no reason to ask who. "When?"

Gregory waved his hand. "Hours ago. Emma said a warrior—who, she dinna ken—came to her bothy with orders to bring Megan to me."

"Search the keep and castle," Daniel shouted to everyone in the great hall. "Megan Mackenzie is missing."

"I doona ken how they got her out."

Daniel placed his hand on Gregory's shoulder. "She may still be here. Perhaps they hid her and are waiting for the keep to settle down before taking her away."

The laird shook his head. "That sounds ridiculous even to me."

Men scattered from the great hall. The search was on.

MEGAN HAD BEEN tied to a tree near where Anthony and the hated Gunn had made camp. Thankfully, the pain in her head had subsided so she could at least think about her dilemma.

Obviously, the warrior who came for her in Emma's bothy was not one of the Makenzie men. Since she was not familiar with them all, she didn't know he was not one of them.

She also thought about the hole in the castle wall. She'd walked around the castle many times, both with Gregory and Beth, and never saw a hole before. Had it been dug out of the wall recently, and for the purpose of dragging her away?

She'd also come to the conclusion that the so-called attack was to allow a distraction while they dragged her off. She and Emma had questioned the indifference of the battle. No Mackenzie injuries, which was good, and only a few Gunn injuries, with one somewhat serious warrior who was giving Emma a hard time.

Sinclair walked over to her and squatted in front of her. "Ye shouldn't have run from me, lass. Ye were promised to The Gunn and our trip to Edinburgh to see the king will straighten it all out."

"Ye can make all the betrothal agreements ye want to, Anthony, but Gregory and I are legally married by the church. This is a waste of time."

Anthony's face softened for a minute. "Did they hurt ye lass? They were told no' to cause ye any harm."

Megan shifted. "Well if ye consider being dragged through a brick wall and then hit o'er the head with something strong enough to knock ye out, then yer men dinna obey yer orders."

Ignoring her remarks, he stood. "We'll be cooking rabbits that my men have caught. I will see that ye get some food."

She sighed. "Am I going to be allowed to take care of my needs and clean myself up?"

He nodded. "Aye. We doona mean to make this hard on ye."

Megan gave a brittle laugh. "Perhaps ye can have someone clean up the back of my head. 'Tis sure I am that there is dried blood there."

Anthony stood and walked over to one of the warriors. It might have been the one who took her, she wasn't sure since by the time she got to the point where she might have been able to identify her captors, they knocked her out.

He waved his hands around, shouting at the man, turning and pointing at Megan. He then walked off and pulled a warrior aside and spoke with him. The warrior looked in Megan's direction. He nodded at Sinclair and walked over to her.

He also squatted in front of her. "I'm to take ye to the nearby creek so ye can do what ye need to do."

"I will need a cloth to clean myself up."

The warrior, no more than a lad, nodded, left her, spoke with Sinclair and returned to her with a piece of linen. He untied her from the tree and helped her up.

They walked in silence away from the camp. She was dizzy, whether from the smack on the head, or what had happened to her in the last few hours she didn't know.

Now that she was able to think clearly, she wondered how soon after she was taken that Gregory found her missing. If he thought she was still working with Emma, he would have no reason to seek her out until it was time for the evening meal.

She looked up, assuming from the position of the sun that it was getting close to that time. Would he come after her? Would he be glad to be rid of a wife who was only a duty? Her heart said no, but her aching head had its doubts.

She felt better after taking care of her needs and then washing in the creek. After cleaning herself, she dipped the cloth in the creek and handed it to the warrior. "Can ye please clean the injury on my head?"

The young warrior stepped back, his eyes wide. "I doona ken how to do that."

Megan sighed. "All I need ye to do is place this on my head and see that all the dried blood is off. I tried the best I could, but I need someone else to finish it up."

He reluctantly took the cloth from her and patted the area. She wasn't convinced that he got rid of all the blood, but it would have to do.

They walked back to the camp. He settled her down in front of the tree and tied her. It wasn't as secure as it had been before, but any likelihood of her escaping was slim. She had no idea where she was and wandering around by herself was more dangerous than the situation she was in.

She dozed for a short time, it seemed, based on the position of the sun once again. Hopefully, the knock she took on her head was not something serious. She knew from working with Emma that head injuries could be dangerous.

The Gunn squatted down in front of her with a flat piece of wood holding some roasted rabbit. Although she would have liked to push it away, her stomach reminded her it needed food if she was to remain strong through this.

He held out the meat. "I am happy to offer food to my soon-to-be wife."

"I am no' yer soon-to-be anything." Still, she took the food.

CHAPTER TWENTY

THEY SEARCHED EVERY inch of the keep, with Gregory going from worry to panic to anger. He couldn't believe neither he nor Daniel had figured out that the Gunn and Sinclair attack was not a serious one. They'd had their doubts about it, but it never occurred to him that it was a ruse to grab Megan.

"Laird!" One of the warriors ran up to them, taking deep breaths. "We discovered how The Gunn got Megan out of the castle."

Daniel and Gregory turned at the same time. "Show me," Gregory said.

As a group they raced to the kitchen, out the back door, past the garden and a little more than halfway down the back wall where a warrior stood. They came to an abrupt halt. Gregory squatted and looked at the hole that had been broken into the wall.

He reached out and ran his finger over dried blood. "Her skin was scraped." The rage at his wife being so mishandled had his heart thumping.

Someone would pay.

He stood and placed his hands on his hips, then turned to Daniel. "If they are traveling in a group, which they most likely are, they canno' travel verra fast. I'm going after her."

Daniel reached out and grabbed his arm. "I have a feeling

they are taking her to Edinburgh."

"Why there?" Gregory asked.

"I received word last week that the king was traveling from London to Edinburgh in an apparent show of power. 'Twas probably why Sinclair and Gunn decided to grab her now. 'Tis a much shorter trip to Edinburgh than London."

"I doona ken what proof they have come up with to annul our marriage, especially after we saw the king's order, which we are certain was false," Gregory growled.

Daniel shook his head. "If they are so determined to get their way that they forged a king's order, 'tis an easy thing to do anything they want in order to break yer vows."

Gregory started to walk away from the wall toward the keep. Daniel grabbed his arm. "I will go with ye. Having a Clan Chief speak for ye might be more convincing."

Gregory shook his head. "Nay, I have our marriage certificate signed by the priest. The king canno' ignore that. And with both of us gone 'tis too dangerous. I still doona trust The Gunn."

Daniel nodded. "Aye." He studied the hole in the wall. "Ye are right," He turned to the two warriors who stood with them. "Get men here immediately and get this hole fixed. Also check the rest of the castle walls and make sure there is nothing else that needs attending."

Gregory left Daniel explaining to the men what needed to be done and jogged the steps up to his bedchamber. His stomach fell when he saw all of Megan's things. He would get her back and make sure The Gunn and The Sinclair received their just punishment.

Broken bones and swords to their middles came to mind.

A great deal of blood.

He took the time to pack his grooming items, along with clothes he would need to appear before the king. He rummaged through one of his trunks, all the way to the bottom where he had placed their marriage certificate.

Once he had everything he would need, he brought his satchel to the stable to have the stable lad tack up his horse and fasten the satchel to the saddle.

Then he strode to the kitchen and talked to Jemima, the cheerful and helpful cook into packing food for him. He had no intention of taking time to do anything except track his wife.

He found Daniel in his solar, looking out the window. He turned as Gregory entered the room. "Ready to leave?"

"Aye."

"I still believe ye would have more influence with the king if I was with ye."

"Nay. Whatever happens, I will return with my wife."

Daniel leaned back in his chair and rested his chin on his thumb and index finger, offering a smile. "Ye love her."

After a moment, Gregory nodded. "Aye. It started out as a vow and obligation, but I love the lass. Megan is my wife and will remain my wife, even if I must go against the king."

"Just be careful, mon. Ye doona want to end up in the king's dungeon."

Gregory laughed. "Nay."

He hurried from the keep and took the reins from the lad. He swung his leg over Apex's back and settled into the saddle, determination in his heart.

MEGAN HAD BEEN hours on the horse, and was weary. Thankfully they hadn't tied her hands because it would have made it difficult to ride. However, the entire day she'd been surrounded by warriors, so there was no escaping.

While they rode, she thought about appearing before the king, which was apparently Anthony's idea. She didn't think she would be looking appropriate to stand before the king. The dress she wore when they took her was not only wrinkled, but the apron covering it that she aways wore when she helped Emma had spots of blood from the warrior they were trying to keep settled so Emma could examine his legs. She'd felt a snag in her dress when they pulled her through the cement hole, so most likely her dress had been torn. And her hair had fallen out of the topknot she'd put it in earlier in the day. That might be Sinclair's plan: to bring her before the king looking dirty and disheveled to show him how she was not being provided for.

She was relieved to see that they had stopped for the night. They didn't seem at all concerned about Gregory coming after her, which she knew in her heart he would.

She looked around their settlement. Behind her was a cluster of trees. In a short time, she would have to relieve herself. Since no one came to help her off the horse, she sat there and watched Anthony and The Gunn argue. She looked around the group, who appeared to ignore her and, growing bored, helped herself off the horse.

She took a seat on a tree stump and viewed the activity. Gunn and Anthony were enjoying their usual whisky while the men traveling with them set up the camp. If she waited long enough, mayhap the two men would be unable to chase her, or even realized she had run.

Her shoulders slumped. She would be putting herself in quite a bit of danger if she tried to escape. She had no horse and wasn't even sure where she would go or even in which direction.

Stories of brigands attacking women and using them made her decision. She would not try to escape, but mayhap the best thing would be to try her best to slow them down, giving Gregory time to find them.

She shook her skirts off and headed toward a cluster of bushes just as she heard a shout from Anthony. "Where do ye think ye are going, lass?"

Megan turned and placed her hands on her hips and huffed. "I need a place to take care of my needs."

The Gunn waved at one of the warriors who stood and walked toward Megan. "I will take ye, lass."

As they walked away, she heard Anthony say, "Ye will need to keep that one in place, ye ken. A fist once in a while would be good."

Her stomach cramped at his words. If Gregory didn't make it in time for her to be swept away by The Gunn—or if he didn't come after her at all—her life would become hell. But then she reassured herself that Gregory loved her, even though he'd never said it. He would not let her go and she had faith in him that he was right now heading to Edinburgh to stop the nonsense.

The farther into the woods they walked, the more the sounds of running water brought a smile to her face. She really needed to clean up. Once she did what she needed to do, she walked toward the young man. "I need to find that creek or stream I can hear."

He looked surprised. "I doona ken, my lady. The Sinclair only said to bring ye to the bushes to…" His words drifted off as his face grew in color. "I'm no' sure."

Megan sighed. "I doubt verra much if that source of water is large enough for me to swim away if that is yer concern."

The lad nodded. "Aye. I'm no' sure where it is, but I think we can find it."

They walked for a short time, following the sound of the water splashing. Eventually they found a nice-sized creek. Megan knelt on the edge of the water and scooped as large an amount as she could into her hands.

She smiled as she bathed her face with the fresh, cool water. She washed her hands and arms, and then did the best she could with the smears of blood on her apron.

Once they returned to the group, Sinclair waved her over. "Doona be so sad, lass. Ye will be marrying a wealthy mon." He grinned at The Gunn. "Especially since he gets yer dowry."

Her breath caught. "What dowry?"

Sinclair waved his hand at her. "The one yer da paid to Robert when ye married."

The Gunn grinned and nudged Sinclair in the ribs. "And which he ne'er saw."

She was stunned at his words. Even though she assumed there had been a dowry as there always was, since Robert never mentioned it, she thought that like most wives she had no say in how it was used and or spent. But now, according to The Gunn, Robert never got the dowry when they married.

She narrowed her eyes. "If there is such a dowry, it must go to Gregory Mackenzie. *My husband.*"

Sinclair swayed on the rock where he sat. "Nay. Ye canno' be married to Gregory Mackenzie because I dinna approve it."

"I dinna need yer approval since ye are no relation to me."

He attempted to slam his hand down on the rock, but missed and would have tumbled to the ground if The Gunn didn't grab his arm and pull him back up.

Once he straightened up, he said, "Aye. I am yer laird. I decide who ye shall marry."

Megan bent at the waist and said in a soft, determined voice, "Laird Daniel Mackenzie is my laird."

Sinclair waved her off and looked over at the lad who had brought her to the bushes and creek. "Take her away and tie her to one of those trees."

The young warrior took her by the arm and walked her to a small tree. She sat and he said, "I need to get the cord to tie ye up with." He started to walk away and turned back. "Doona run away."

She had to smile at the lad. It was a good thing she had already decided that running away was dangerous. He soon returned and wrapped her with the cord, then walked off.

Megan went over in her mind what Anthony had said. So there was a dowry that Robert never received. That probably explained why The Gunn was so insistent in marrying her. He would get the dowry that was meant for Robert. What she couldn't think of an explanation for was the question she'd asked herself many times over: Why was Anthony so anxious to marry her off to The Gunn? What was it in for him if The Gunn got the dowry? They could have had an agreement to split it. And another question was, if Anthony had the dowry, why hadn't he spent it?

Once again her head started to pound, so she pushed all the unanswerable questions from her mind.

It was getting dark when another warrior carried food to her. It was a roasted animal of sorts. With the dimness it was hard to tell what it was. But being hungry, she didn't care and ate the whole thing.

CHAPTER TWENTY-ONE

GREGORY PUSHED HIMSELF, preferring to find Megan's group before they reached Edinburgh. He knew that without an invitation it would be hard to gain an audience with the king. He would prefer to take Megan home without a battle in which she could be hurt.

But if necessary, he would do just that to get his wife back.

He spent the time racing toward Edinburgh thinking about Megan, the wife he had married to fulfill a vow. Things had certainly changed. After saying he'd never find a wife, now he'd discovered he loved a lass and he was sure she loved him as well.

In spite of all his fears, he'd realized that he and Megan could have a good life together. Even if what she said was true and she was barren, all they had to do was take a walk through the village and the area beyond to find children who had lost their parents and whose family members had taken them in but were feeling overwhelmed. They would be more than happy to have someone else care for them. He was sure Megan would be happy to care for them too.

He didn't care whether they had children of their own. All he wanted was Megan, and whatever the cost, he would pay it.

The pounding of horses' hooves sounded behind him. He slowed down, entered the wooded area to his right and withdrew his sword. He was silent as whoever it was approached at a rapid pace.

As they raced by, he recognized three of the warriors from Mackenzie. "Halt!"

The men all drew their swords. Gregory rode out of the wooded area. "What are ye doing here?"

The obvious leader of the group, a warrior named Luke, said, "Looking for ye to keep ye from getting yerself killed."

"I doona need anyone to keep me from getting killed."

"Then let us just say we are here to keep ye from getting lost."

Gregory shook his head. "Ye had better keep up. I have no idea how far The Sinclair has gone, although I have my doubts 'tis verra far, but I would prefer to meet them on the road, and no' in front of the king."

The men turned their horses and took off.

Gloaming had started when Gregory raised his arm as a sign to the warriors to stop. The men all slowed down and formed a circle. "Are we stopping for the night, then?" Luke asked, his horse prancing in place, still anxious to continue on.

"Aye. I am no' familiar with this area since I try to avoid Edinburgh as much as possible. 'Twould be verra hard to find our way in the dark." He rested his forearm on his saddle. "I doona think The Sinclair will travel at night either. We shall make camp, find something to cook and leave at first light."

⸎

So CERTAIN WAS Megan that Gregory was coming for her, that she did everything in her power to slow them down. She complained about her stomach hurting. She asked to stop to relieve herself numerous times.

She toed her boot off, and then a few furlongs later told Sinclair that it dropped off and she hadn't noticed.

One of their men returned with the boot and handed it to her with a smirk on his face.

"I doona ken what ye are thinking, lass, but yer so-called husband willna be coming for ye. He has no use for ye," Anthony said. He waved a paper in front of her. "I have it here in his own handwriting that he only married ye to fulfill a vow made to Robert, and he releases ye to marry Gunn."

Megan's mouth went dry and her stomach muscles tightened. Nay, she dinna believe it. She raised her chin. "I would see that paper." She stuck her hand out.

With a smirk on his face, Anthony handed the paper to Megan. She was unable to read, but since Robert's uncle was so unconcerned about the missive's contents that he gladly handed it over, she had to assume what it said was true.

She blinked rapidly as she gave it back to him, her hand shaking.

So it was true. What she'd always feared. Gregory didn't care enough for her to keep her from marrying The Gunn. He had only been doing his duty and now with someone else wanting her hand, he gladly turned her over. Then he could get back to his normal life that she had interrupted.

Probably because she was barren. Although, with how much she and Gregory enjoyed the marriage bed, mayhap she was not barren.

She tried to push it out of her mind but it was very confusing. Once she was settled in whatever keep she ended up in, she would seek out the midwife and learn all about being barren and what she could do to correct it.

Nay. She mentally shook her head. She would settle in no keep except the Mackenzie. And if she were forced to marry The Gunn she would do whatever it took to avoid the marriage bed. She shivered at the thought.

No man would ever compare to Gregory. She did feel a bit remorseful that Robert's attentions did not compare to Gregory's but her husband did seem to spend a lot more time making sure she didn't suffer any pain when he entered her.

She sighed and let her thoughts wander. Mayhap the paper

Anthony showed her was a fake. Daniel and Gregory had thought the king's order was a fake. She smiled and felt herself beginning to perk up. Yes, that was it. They were lying to her, taking a chance on the fact that she couldn't read.

She shut up the voice in her head that said it was true. What it came down to was—did she trust Gregory?

Yes.

Maybe.

They stopped for the night and she heard The Gunn and Anthony grousing to each other that all the stops Megan required had slowed them down.

She pretended to be asleep to hear what else they said, hoping they would mention the letter that Gregory supposedly signed was fake.

Tired from all the travel she was unused to, she fell into a restless slumber and heard no more until the sounds of the men rising and getting their horses ready told her it was time to go.

⟫⟫⟫⟪⟪⟪

GREGORY KICKED ONE of the warriors traveling with him in the foot. "Time to get up."

John rolled over. "'Tis still dark."

"Aye, and time to leave."

The men slowly rose, stretching and relieving themselves at the end of the clearing where they had slept.

Once Gregory had shared what was left of the bannocks and cheese that Jemima had sent with him, each warrior drank from their own wineskin, draining the rest of the ale they'd carried. Then they were off to another day of hard riding.

To Gregory's way of thinking they were still days away from Edinburg. He just prayed that he and Daniel were correct and Sinclair and Gunn had dragged Megan there.

If he found she was there, he would tear the city apart to find her.

As the day wore on, the weather grew ominous. Gregory looked at the sky once they rode away from the two mountains that had blocked their view. "This doesna look good, lads."

They all looked up and grimaced. Dark clouds had gathered quite a bit since they'd resumed their journey that morning.

"Looks to me as if we're in for a good storm."

Gregory sighed. "We'll continue until the rain forces us to stop." The last thing they needed was to be held up by bad weather. Although, if they were hampered so were Sinclair and his men.

Not wanting to travel in wet clothes, once the rain began they took cover under a grouping of trees. The men were silent, leaving Gregory with his own thoughts.

He smiled, thinking of how Megan had wanted a marriage of convenience when they first wed. He continued to be confused when Megan had said that Robert had criticized her for a lack of enthusiasm in the bedchamber. It had occurred to Gregory the first time they made love that Megan was merely a woman who needed more attention before her body was prepared for a man. 'Twas not a rare problem and he'd noticed that as time went on, she didn't need as much time as she had in the beginning.

His wife.

Even thinking about her brought a smile to his face. She was sweet, kind, helpful and made him laugh. As a warrior, he had decided back when he and Robert made their vow that he would not take a wife. And the children who would follow. Leaving a family of his to fend for itself with all the difficulties of life scared him. But all that had changed when he met and married Megan.

He looked up at the sky which continued to bring the rain that hampered their journey. It truly didn't matter to him if the king decided to break their marriage vows and give Megan to The Gunn.

Megan Mackenzie was his and she would remain his. If he had to burn down the Gunn castle to get her back, that was precisely what he would do.

And then take great pleasure in killing the man. Slowly. And painfully.

CHAPTER TWENTY-TWO

T HE GUNN RAISED his hand just as rain began to fall. "We will stop here for the night."

Worn out from the trip, Megan looked up in the semi-darkness and, after wiping the water from her eyes, she could make out an inn.

It was not large, but it looked welcoming with the sight of several windows, lights from candles and most likely a fireplace, bringing a smile to her face. She shivered, anxious to get out of the rain and her wet clothes. Hopefully she would have her own room and be able to lay her things in front of a fire.

One of the men came over and dragged her off her horse. Without notice, she lost her balance and fell into a mud puddle.

"See here, Micah, that is my future wife ye are tossing around like a bag of flour. Help her up." The Gunn gave his order and before she was barely on her feet, the man had disappeared inside.

"I will need a bedchamber for me and my wife." Gunn pounded the counter in the inn.

Megan stepped right up to him. "I am no' this mon's wife, and will ne'er be. I demand my own room."

The Gunn growled and raised his hand to strike her, when Anthony stopped him. "We need her looking uninjured when we appear before the king. What ye do after that is yer business."

The innkeeper looked back and forth between them just as a well-rounded woman with a cheerful look about her, who must have been his wife, walked up to them. "The young lady will have her own chamber, Marcus." She nodded to the man behind the counter.

Weariness, fright, and missing her husband brought Megan to tears. The woman standing next to the innkeeper walked around the counter and put her arm around her. "Come with me, lass. I'll get ye a nice room and a hot meal."

"I object!" The Gunn said.

The woman just ignored him and ushered Megan upstairs to one of the chambers.

She was shivering and feeling absolutely miserable. She missed Gregory so much it only made her cry harder. If he was here, he would peel her wet clothes off her cold body, dry her in a cloth, then wrap her in a blanket, and place her on his lap as they sat in front of the brazier. She would lay her head on his warm chest and everything would be right with her world. Thinking that her world might never be right again, she cried harder.

"I doona ken what is wrong with ye lass, but I doona believe for one minute that the man downstairs is yer husband."

Megan wiped her nose on her wet sleeve and shook her head. "Nay. My husband is Gregory Mackenzie. I love him so much and these men downstairs are going to the king in Edinburgh to have my marriage annulled. I ken Gregory is coming after me, but I'm afraid he will arrive too late."

The woman tsked and shook her head. "I canno' get involved with my customers' troubles, or we would lose our business. However, if ye wish to scratch out a note for yer husband, I will be happy to pass it along to him should he stop here."

Megan's shoulders slumped. "I canno' write."

"'Tis no' a problem. My husband can write. He had to learn to be able to make sure we were no' being cheated." She stopped to grin. "Now let me help ye out of those wet clothes. I'll bring ye a cloth to dry yerself and a nightshift my daughter left behind when she married her husband."

"Thank ye so much. Ye are so kind."

The woman patted her on the arm and left the room, which Megan figured was to get the drying cloth and nightshift. She started to peel her clothes off, but had problems with unfastening the bodice, so she stood waiting for the innkeeper's wife. She didn't want to sit anywhere and wet the furniture.

She felt heartened by the innkeeper's wife's help. She really should ask the woman her name. She was so cheerful and friendly.

The chances of Gregory stopping at the inn might not be great, but since this was the only inn they'd past since they left Mackenzie, he might guess that they stopped here for no other reason than to have a soft bed to lie on.

They had avoided all the villages on their journey because Anthony didn't want to waste time—mostly, she was sure, because he knew Gregory was on their trail. Her husband was an excellent tracker and in the short time she'd been at the Mackenzie keep she had heard stories about his unlimited ability to search out brigands and other miscreants.

He would come for her.

A soft knock at the door caught her attention before it opened. "Here we are, dear." The rosy-cheeked woman held garments in her arms.

"May I please ken yer name? I am Megan Mackenzie, wife of Gregory Mackenzie."

"Mrs. Anna Bruce, dear. Mr. Marcus Bruce is my husband." She held out her arms. "I have some things here for ye." She laid them on the bed and turned to her. "If ye turn around, I will help ye get undressed. I wish I could offer ye a hot bath, but I doona have anyone to carry up the water."

"That is fine, Mrs. Bruce. Just getting out of these wet clothes and into something dry will help." She turned so the woman could help her.

One she had removed her clothes and dried herself with a

piece of linen, and slid the nightshift over her, she felt many times better.

"I will take yer things and put them by the fireplace downstairs so they can dry." She pointed to the small brazier in the room. "I will have my grandson, who lives here with us, fill that with some peat to get ye warmed up."

"Thank ye so much."

Once the woman left, carrying her wet garments, Megan climbed onto the bed and pulled the bedcovers up over her. She'd been shivering since she entered the inn, and for the first time she felt a bit of warmth.

Now that her brain was not frozen, she turned her attention to what The Gunn had said downstairs. Trying to pass her off as his wife! If only she could talk Mrs. Bruce into letting her stay here, but the woman was right. She could not interfere with her guests or they would lose a lot of business if word spread.

Loud voices and laughter and what sounded like someone falling came from the room next door. At the same time there was a knock on her door. Afraid it was Anthony or Gunn, she walked softly across the floor and leaned up against the door. "Who is there?"

"My lady, I am the innkeeper's son and I bring ye a tray for yer dinner."

Breathing a sigh of relief, she opened the door and he handed her the tray. She thanked him and said, "There is quite a bit of noise in the room next to me."

He nodded. "Aye, two of the men who arrived with ye are in there for the night. 'Tis sorry I am if they are disturbing ye."

"Nay. I will just lock the door."

Since they had all arrived together, the lad looked a tad confused but shrugged and bid her good night.

She finished the wonderful bowl of mutton stew, along with freshly baked bread and the cup of ale that had accompanied the meal.

More tired than ever, she crawled into bed and fell instantly asleep.

A loud crash from the room next to her woke her out of a sound sleep. Without thought, she reached out for Gregory and felt only a cold empty space. Immediately, she remembered where she was. Her fear and sadness were slowly turning to anger. How dare Robert take her from her home and drag her off to see the king and attempt to have her marriage annulled.

Loud voices had her stepping out of bed. The fire in the brazier was low, and it was cold in the room. But that didn't stop her from placing her ear against the wall.

'Twas Anthony and The Gunn arguing. And from their voices it sounded as though they had quite a bit to drink.

She raced back to the bed and grabbed the covers, covered herself and returned to the wall.

"I still doona understand why ye get half the dowry when yer getting Megan. She's a comely lass, and I'm sure after a few smacks she'll settle down and ye'll have a good wife." She sucked in a breath at the sound of Anthony's voice.

"Shut ye mouth, Sinclair. I think the king would be interested to ken ye had Robert killed in that small skirmish just so ye could claim Megan's dowry as her husband and laird."

That answered a question she'd had for a while: what was in it for Robert's uncle to be so insistent she marry The Gunn. Then as the words sunk into her brain, her stomach churned. Her husband's death had been planned? She sucked in a deep breath and covered her mouth. He'd been murdered!

Too sickened to continue listening, she returned to her bed. She'd always known Anthony was a greedy, horrible man. From the little she'd heard of the muffled conversation, somehow The Gunn found out what Anthony had done and the price of his silence was her as a wife and half her dowry.

Amid tears, she offered more prayers for Robert's soul. And God forgive her, she cursed Anthony's soul.

CHAPTER TWENTY-THREE

GREGORY SPENT HIS time thinking about his marriage and leaning against the doorway of the abandoned bothy they had found to avoid the rain. He was still quite surprised that he was indeed married. Had he known how satisfying it could be, he might have not been so against it.

Except not every lass was Megan. He had to smile when images of his wife flashed before him as she had settled in Castle Leod. She and Beth had seemed to get along well, which was very important since she was the laird's wife.

Megan also seemed interested in helping Emma with ill clan members.

Megan had also gone from a nervous, reluctant bed partner to an enthusiastic one. He felt his cods stiffen as he thought about how, given his marriage was begun in an unusual way, it had turned out quite well.

"Ye better get some sleep, Mackenzie, instead of pinning after yer wife." Luke grinned at him as he rolled over.

As much as Gregory wanted to lash out at the man, 'twas true he was thinking about Megan. About missing her. Caring for her. Protecting her.

And loving her.

The next morning Gregory was up and ready to be on their way, kicking the men on the feet to get moving. If they rode hard all day today, despite the rough terrain in front of them, they should reach the outskirts of Edinburgh by the end of the next day.

He'd really thought he would have caught up to Sinclair and his group by now, and was beginning to become anxious that perhaps the man had not brought Megan to Edinburgh, and he would never see her again.

Then he shook himself. The Gunn was laird of his clan and it was not likely that his determination to steal his wife would include actually leaving the country.

After a breakfast of food they'd gotten in the last village, wandering off their path for a while, they rode. Hard and fast.

A few hours passed and they came across an inn. Since Gregory was anxious for a hot meal, he held up his arm for the men to stop. "A good hot meal will hold us until we reach Edinburgh. And the horses could use some food and a good rub down."

They left their horses in the stable and entered the inn. A man was behind the counter at the end of the room. "Do ye wish a room for the night?"

"Nay," Gregory said. "Just a good, hot meal and then we must get back on our horses."

The man nodded and the five of them took a seat at a table. The innkeeper brought them each an ale, and shortly after that a woman who apparently was his wife entered the room with a trayful of steaming bowls and bread. Gregory licked his lips. She laid the food down and put two loaves of still-warm bread on the table.

She paused for a moment and studied him, but then walked off.

"She's a bit old for ye, Gregory," Ethan said with a grin.

Gregory grunted and dug into his food. I didn't matter to him how old any lass was. All he wanted was his Megan.

They ate in silence and all requested a second helping. Once their appetites were satisfied the woman returned to the table, her hands clasped at her abundant waist. "Would ye like some tea?"

They all shook their heads. Gregory said, "Ye can bring us another round of ale and then we must be off."

Again she hesitated and studied him for a minute. "Are ye headed to Edinburgh?"

Gregory leaned back in his chair and crossed his arms over his chest. "Aye."

She fumbled with her hands for a few minutes, and he said, "Out with it, lass. Ye've been trying verra hard to no' say something to me since I arrived."

She reached into the pocket of her apron and pulled out a necklace.

Gregory leaned forward and took the necklace from her hand. Looking up at the woman, he said, "Where did ye get this?"

"It depends. What is ye name?"

"Gregory Mackenzie of Castle Leod."

A bright smile broke out on her flushed face. "I am Mrs. Bruce, wife to Marcus Bruce, the owner of this inn. A lass named Megan Mackenzie gave this to me and said to watch for ye. She is headed to the king in Edinburgh with men she doesna want to be with."

Gregory broke into a sweat as he looked at his mother's necklace that he'd given to Megan after their wedding ceremony. It meant a great deal to him and to Megan, so he knew she would only give it to this woman if she was in dire straits.

He jumped up and kissed the woman on the cheek. "Thank ye so much. Ye have no idea how happy this makes me." He paused for a moment. "Was she well?"

"Aye. But no' happy. One of the men with her tried to tell me she was his wife and requested they share a bedchamber."

Gregory growled.

The woman nodded. "She stood right there and said, 'Nay, I am no' his wife.' I came out from the kitchen just as she said that. I told my husband she was to have her own bedchamber." She shook her head. "I dinna like the looks of the mon, or the other one who was with him."

Ethan tapped him on the arm. "What is it?"

Gregory smiled and looked down at his palm. "Megan and I went to the village one day and she saw this necklace. When she wasn't looking, I bought it and gave it to her that night." He slipped it into his pouch.

"And ye got a good reward for it, aye?"

Gregory slapped him on the back of his head. "Doona talk about my wife."

They all threw some money on the table and left. Gregory's spirits lifted because he had proof that they were going in the right direction.

Stay strong, Megan. I am coming for ye.

MEGAN IMMEDIATELY DISLIKED Edinburgh. It was smelly, crowded and hot, even though 'twas Fall. It must have been all the people packed into the city.

They passed through the gate at the wall after being questioned by one of the guards stationed there. She was very surprised that neither Anthony nor Gunn told the guard they were off to see the king.

That was very strange. She rode her horse up next to The Gunn. "Why did ye no' tell the guard ye were here to see the king?"

He stared straight ahead and she wasn't sure he heard her until he said, "'Twas none of his business." Then he turned to her. "And none of yer business, either, wife."

"Doona call me 'wife'."

He threw his head back and laughed. She dropped back to her prior place and covered her mouth and nose with her arisaid trying to keep the smell from her.

It appeared that Anthony had been in Edinburgh before since he seemed to navigate the streets quite well.

After what seemed like hours of smells and noise they arrived at Holyroodhouse, the king's home and headquarters. Megan was exhausted and all she wanted was to have Gregory find her and bring her home.

Home.

She almost cried with the pictures in her mind of her home. Where Gregory lived and took care of her. Where she was accepted by the other clan members. Where Gregory bought her that beautiful necklace that she left with the woman at the inn.

She noticed that Gunn and Anthony were arguing with the guards in front of the king's home. She wondered why they did not pull out the king's order that she should marry The Gunn.

There was something wrong about this whole thing. She was beginning to believe there was no king's order for her to marry him. Before she was able to think too long and hard on this, a woman walked up to her. "Come with me, lass."

"Where are we going?"

The woman didn't answer her, but practically dragged her down the corridor.

"Who are ye?"

Still no answer, but continued on their way.

They eventually stopped in front of an old, battered door. The woman fished a key off the piece of leather hanging around her neck. She opened the door and pointed at the room. "Yer bath is ready. Someone will be here to help ye dress."

"I have no other clothing," Megan said as the door closed in her face. She rubbed her palms up and down her arms, looking around. The room was damp, but mostly from its age, but there was a slight amount of warmth coming from a fireplace against one wall.

She walked toward the fireplace. A bathtub sat in front of it, filled with scented water. She put her hand in the water. It was warm. Despite not wanting to do anything that Anthony and Gunn had to do with it, she loved the idea of getting out of her dirty clothes and cleaning her body.

As she began to undress, she noticed a woman's kirtle and léine laying on the bed. She had no idea how he had arranged it, but Robert's uncle had someone here at the king's residence working with him.

Most likely the rude woman.

CHAPTER TWENTY-FOUR

GREGORY AND HIS men were barely past the guards at the gate to Edinburgh when he remembered why he hated the place. Give him country air anytime over the smells, smoke and crowds of a city.

The guards weren't too happy to share the location of Holyroodhouse. Gregory shook his head as they rode off. He was certain there were plenty of guards at the king's residence to protect him.

"First we need to put our names in to speak with the king. Then we must find an inn where we can obtain a bedchamber so we can all clean up. It won't be necessary for ye to be dressed formally since ye won't be standing before king, but guarding my back while I stand before him."

They rode a short way before stopping at a clean-looking inn. "Run inside and see if they have a room or two," Gregory said to Luke.

The man was out within minutes, a big smile on his face. "Aye, he has two rooms and the smells coming from the kitchen are making my stomach verra happy."

The men rode their horses to the stable behind the inn. Once they left instructions to the stable lads, Gregory grabbed his satchel and headed inside. Luke was right, the smells were wonderful.

A young lass of no more than ten years, most likely a daughter of the innkeeper, showed them upstairs to their rooms. "Lass, can ye arrange to send a message to the king's residence?"

Her eyes grew wide. "The king?"

"Aye. If ye get it to Holyroodhouse fast, there will be a coin for ye."

"I must ask my da."

Gregory nodded. "Go ask him and also please request a bath be sent up while I write the note."

She scurried away and Gregory looked around. "Based on what the woman at the inn told us, The Gunn and his group should have arrived only a few hours before us. I ken it is impossible to be granted an audience with His Majesty quickly, so I think we have time."

"What sort of note will ye be sending?" John asked as he flopped down on the bed.

"Get off there with yer dirty clothes on," Gregory said. "I am going to tell the king to expect to hear from The Gunn and The Sinclair and I wish to be granted an audience at the same time because what they will be discussing directly affects me."

He started to remove his clothes when three men carried in a bathtub and buckets of water. Once they filled the tub about halfway, the young girl came back to the room.

"Aye sir, my da says I can take a note to the Holyroodhouse if ye give me another coin for him, too." She smiled, which made Gregory smile back.

"Aye lass. Once ye return from the king's residence I will give ye two coins. One for ye and one for yer da. Do ye have any parchment or other type of paper and a writing instrument I can use?"

She looked confused.

"Ask yer da. Or mam."

She hurried away, the sound of her feet racing down the stairs.

"Ye can all take a break and sip on an ale downstairs while I enjoy my bath." Gregory waved them off.

MEGAN PACED THE floor in the bedchamber she'd been given. It had been two days since they'd arrived at Edinburgh. She'd been allowed out of the room twice a day with two of The Gunn's men to take a walk outside.

As much as she'd loved getting out of the room, she was always anxious to get back because of the crowds. The place smelled atrocious and people pushed and shoved to get where they were going.

And so many times she had to duck or else be doused with a bucket of God-knew-what from a window.

All she wanted right now was Gregory's arms wrapped around her and a trip back to Castle Leod. She had grown to love the place and the people she'd met there. Beth was very helpful and kind.

The clan healer, Emma, had helped her learn much more in healing than she'd already known. Her thoughts turned to the battle Emma had been having with the Gunn warrior who was trying to have her let him return to the battle, even though it appeared he had a broken leg, or two. She smiled thinking that the warrior had no idea how determined Emma was when it came to her healing skills. He might be a strong warrior, but Emma could certainly hold her own with the men.

Her thoughts drifted to The Gunn's and Anthony's drunken conversation she'd overheard when they stayed at the inn. She had always wondered why Robert had been slain in that minor skirmish. He'd been a strong and wonderful warrior who had fought numerous battles and rarely ever suffered an injury.

No matter how things turned out for her—and she prayed very hard every day that she would return to Castle Leod with Gregory—she fully intended to let the king know about Robert's death.

A slight knock on the door drew her away from her thoughts. Without invitation, The Gunn opened the door and looked her up and down. "Ye will do. When ye are married to me, ye will burn all yer clothes and have new ones made that appeal to me."

Megan drew herself up. "I will ne'er be married to ye."

He strode across the room and leaned into her face. "Once we are married—and we *will* be married—ye will hold yer tongue or spend a great deal of time recovering."

She shivered, praying once again that Gregory had seen Mrs. Bruce and received her necklace.

The Gunn grabbed her arm and practically dragged her from the room. "We are expected at Holyroodhouse to see the king. Ye will behave yerself or pay the price once we leave." He put his hand to her back and pushed her.

Megan stumbled, but caught herself before she fell. The Gunn continued to drag her down the stairs and out of the inn. There was a carriage a few feet from the door with a very bored driver sitting at the top.

The Gunn shoved her into the carriage. Anthony was already inside and caught her before she hit the floor of the vehicle.

She sat across from him and smoothed out the garment they had provided her. At least they'd gotten enough petticoats that once she put her arisaid on she felt covered. Somehow they had managed to clean the garment, and she was thankful they did not make her wear the Gunn plaid to appear before the king.

Once they arrived and climbed out of the carriage, she suddenly felt extremely nervous. She looked up at the building and realized she could very well leave there annulled from Gregory and married to The Gunn.

She broke into a sweat and felt as though she would faint. Once more The Gunn grabbed her arm and moved her forward.

They were left waiting in a small room for over an hour. Finally, a courtier arrived and said the king would see them. Again Megan felt as though she would faint and her legs felt like water.

They arrived in front of King George II. If Megan had not been so terrified she would have given the king more notice. But to her he was the man who could destroy her life.

"What is this nonsense that is brought before me? Why can't you Highlanders keep from fighting all the time? You take up my time to resolve issues you should settle yourselves."

Sinclair bowed before the king and said, "I am sorry to take up yer time, Yer Majesty, but this is an issue that only ye can resolve."

The king said nothing, but waved him on.

"My nephew, Robert Sinclair, Laird of Sinclair clan died un-expectedly in a minor battle. As is the law, his wife, Megan Sinclair came under my protection."

The king didn't comment only waved for him to continue.

"In order to keep my niece Megan Sinclair protected and cared for, I arranged a betrothal agreement between her and Laird Stephen Angus Gunn."

"And why am I involved in this?" The king asked.

"Because apparently my nephew made an agreement with Gregory Mackenzie to marry his wife should he die."

"And?" The king said.

"Gregory Mackenzie kidnapped my niece and stole her away." He fumbled a bit and withdrew the fake message. "I have here in my possession a letter Mackenzie wrote himself saying he only married the lass to fulfill a vow. He is more than happy to have Your Majesty annul the marriage so she is free to marry Laird Gunn."

Even though Megan believed in her heart that Gregory never wrote that missive, her stomach twisted at hearing those words spoken out loud.

Her head jerked up as the door to the room opened with such force it slammed against the wall. Fighting off two guards, Gregory stormed into the room. Her heart leapt in her chest and she felt weak at the knees. He came to an abrupt stop, took one look at Megan and held out his arms. "Come here, Wife."

With a sob, she wrenched her arm from The Gunn and flew across the room and slammed into Gregory, wrapping her arms and legs around him so tightly it was a miracle the man could breathe. She looked up at him, smiling into his deep blue eyes with love and relief. "Ye came. Thank God."

"I told ye I would no' let ye go." He grinned as he looked down at her, cupping her face in his large, warm hand. "Do ye no' trust me, Wife?"

CHAPTER TWENTY-FIVE

THE GUARDS WHO he had to fight to get into the room attempted to pull them apart. Without success.

"Halt!" The king rose from his seat and pounded on the table in front of him.

Things quieted. The king brushed off his flowing sleeves, sat down, and said to the guards. "Keep guard against the wall."

He then looked at Gregory. "There are better ways to enter a room, Mackenzie."

Gregory kept his arm wrapped around Megan and nodded at the king. "I am verra sorry to have burst through the door like that, but yer guards would no' let me enter."

He frowned. "I told them to expect ye, based on yer missive."

"Aye, but they wanted me to wait until this hearing was finished. I was taking no chances."

The king pointed to Sinclair and Gunn. "These men are insisting that yer wife be taken from ye and given to The Gunn based on a betrothal he signed."

Without thinking, Gregory put Megan behind him. Megan began to whimper. "Yer Majesty, I am aware that women have verra little say in who they marry, but I have here the vow her deceased husband, Robert Sinclair and I made years ago to marry each other's widow in case of our untimely death."

The king placed his hands on the arms of his stately chair. "So ye did marry the lass to fulfill a vow."

Gregory gazed down at Megan who was now back at his side. "Aye. That I did. However, I have since discovered I love the lass and want her for my wife for the rest of my time here on earth."

Sinclair started to speak and the king waved him off. "And how does the lass feel?"

Megan peered up at him with her beautiful wide eyes full of feeling. "I love him, Your Majesty." She spoke to the king but didn't look away from Gregory.

Gregory closed his eyes for a moment. Then squeezed her slightly and looked back at the king. "Whatever note ye have there that says I doona want to keep Megan *Mackenzie* is fake." He reached into his pouch. "I have here the marriage certificate signed by Father Matthew who performed the ceremony. Our union has been blessed by the Church."

The king bowed his head and then looked over at The Gunn and The Sinclair. "I see no reason to annul this marriage."

The two lairds started to speak at once. The king sat forward and the guards against the wall walked up behind the two men. "Cease! My decision has been made."

Gregory was surprised to see Megan raise her hand. It would be better if they made a quick exit and left this blasted city. He prayed she wouldn't say something that gave the king more to think upon.

The king smiled at her as if she was a little girl. "What is it, lass?"

Megan took a deep breath and said, "I have reason to believe Laird Sinclair and Laird Gunn conspired to have my husband, Laird Robert Sinclair, killed."

The king, Gregory, The Gunn, The Sinclair, and all the guards in the room sucked in deep breaths and turned to her.

"Wife, 'tis no' a good idea to say something like that," Gregory whispered while attempting to pull her toward the door.

The king pounded on the table again. "Stop, Mackenzie, the lass has made a very serious charge. I would hear what she has to say."

Megan walked up closer to the king. Gregory was right alongside her, sweating and watching the door.

She told the story of what she'd heard when they stayed in the inn.

The king glared at the two men. Before he could speak, Gregory raised his hand. "Yer Majesty, may I add something?"

He nodded.

"Since I first heard of Robert Sinclair's death, I questioned it. I had no proof or reason to believe these men were involved in his death. However, Laird Robert Sinclair was one of the best, if not *the* best, warrior I ever trained with. I didn't see him a great deal over the years, but I did hear praises from men who had battled with him. Sinclair never had an injury that required the care of a healer.

"But this was a minor skirmish and I always had questions about his death."

Sinclair and Gunn were both shouting, one trying to be heard over the other one.

"This is a very serious matter. The planned death of a Clan Chief will not be tolerated." He looked at the two guards in the room. "Throw them into the dungeon until I can further consider this."

While they were being dragged off, Gunn screamed at Sinclair, "He will get all her money now."

Gregory looked at her. "Ye have money?"

She shrugged "It appears so."

The king turned and frowned at Gregory. "You need to handle your own problems in the Highlands. You are squabbling all the time. I don't like being annoyed with your problems."

Gregory smirked. "Your Majesty, had I handled it myself, both men would be dead."

The king waved his hand. "However you wish to deal with it. For now, you may go, Mackenzie." He looked at Megan. "And take your lovely wife with you."

Gregory grabbed her hand and hauled her out of the room.

He waved to his four warriors who were waiting for him in the outer room to follow them.

They all left as quickly as possible. They went to the stables and Gregory tossed Megan on the back of his horse and swung his leg over. The rest of the men did the same.

"Let's get out of this place as quickly as we can." He tucked Megan onto his lap and moved forward. "We can stop at an inn right outside Edinburgh for the night."

She shook her head. "Nay, husband. I want to go home. I doona want to stop at all."

Gregory looked down at her. "We canno' go straight through. Ye canno' last and neither can the horses."

She sighed and slumped in his arms. "I just want to go home." He could hear the tears in her voice which was ripping him apart.

She wiped her face and looked up at him. "I want to get out of these clothes. And then burn them."

He leaned in closer and said, "I'll be more than happy to get ye out of yer clothes, *mo chridhe*."

She slapped him on the arm. "I mean it, husband. They smell terrible, like someone doused them with perfume."

"Then I have a suggestion. We stop at the inn where ye left yer necklace. Ye can have a bath and I ken Mrs. Bruce would be able to get ye a new set of clothes. Then after a meal, we will stay one night and then we can travel straight through each day until we reach home, if that is what ye want."

Megan closed her eyes and sighed. "Aye. That is exactly what I want."

MEGAN FELT SAFE and protected for the first time in weeks. She'd had her bath, and just as Gregory had said, Mrs. Bruce had clothes for her to wear.

She was in bed, watching her warrior husband remove his clothes and climb into the bath she'd just finished. She loved admiring his strong body, the way the muscles flexed, and…

"Do ye approve of what ye see, lass?" Gregory grinned as he took the washcloth and after rubbing soap on it, washed his body.

"Aye. I do, husband. Now finish up."

He took the quickest bath she'd ever seen anyone take. Of course, she hadn't really seen other people taking baths, but she was sure no one was faster.

After drying, he tossed the linen on the floor and climbed into the bed. "Come here, *mo chridhe*."

She immediately slid over and he gathered her into his arms and held her snugly, his flesh meeting her flesh. "I missed ye."

"Aye. And I missed ye. There was a time I was afraid I would ne'er see ye again."

He pushed the still damp hair off her forehead. "Nay, Megan Mackenzie. Ye will be forced to look at me for the rest of our lives."

She closed her eyes and whispered. "Aye."

He cupped her face in his hands and kissed her, which immediately had her body softening and warming for him. Her flesh prickled at his touch. Within minutes his hands were everywhere, as were hers.

"I love ye so much, Megan. Ye scared me to death when ye disappeared. For that I should have killed The Gunn and The Sinclair instead of the king throwing them in the dungeon."

"I love ye too, husband. Ye have no idea how frightened I was the farther they took me away from ye."

"Enough talk." His hands cupped both her breasts, then gave one of them a good, hard suckle.

A brief shiver ran through her body. "Aye, husband." Megan's voice shook. "That feels so verra good."

She could feel him grin against her breast as he swirled his tongue over her hardened nipple. He kissed his way down her body, and after spreading her legs, he gave her woman's place a good lick.

"Aye!" Her head moved back and forth, and her hands gripped his shoulders. "Keep doing that," she panted.

He watched her, never taking his tongue off the stiffened muscle. Their eyes locked as their breathing came in unison. It didn't take long for her body to tense and break into pieces, her reaction swift and almost violent.

He kissed his way up her body and covered her mouth, his tongue exploring the recesses of her mouth. She could taste herself on his lips as he moved into position. He placed his cock at her entrance and slid in. "Ye are so warm and wet for me, Megan."

She began to move with him and it didn't take long for her to have another spasm and for Gregory pull her even closer, and holding her head, kissing her, releasing his seed into her, with a groan.

After a few minutes while they caught their breath, Gregory said, "Welcome home, Megan Mackenzie."

EPILOGUE

GREGORY'S FACE SCRUNCHED up as he held Megan's hair away from her face while she brought up her dinner from the night before. When she was done, she leaned back on her heels. "Husband, I think I must see Emma. This stomach issue I've had almost since we returned from Edinburgh should be gone by now."

He looked at her carefully. "Aye I agree. I think 'tis time to see what Emma says about this."

They both rose and he gave her a glass of water to rinse her mouth. "I would go with ye, but I've missed so much time with the new warriors that I need to concentrate on them. See what Emma says and mayhap she has a tonic or tisane ye can take to feel better."

She nodded. Once Gregory left the room to break his fast and hurry to the lists, she sat on the bed. She felt so weary lately.

Sometime later, she opened her eyes and realized she had fallen back to sleep after Gregory had left the room. Based on the sun's position, she'd been asleep for a couple of hours.

She didn't mind missing her morning meal because her stomach was still a bit tender. But Beth must wonder where she was. It was her job to assist the Lady of the Manor in various jobs.

She quickly dressed, and reminded herself to see Emma sometime during the day, then she left her bedchamber and looked for Beth.

"There ye are," Beth said with a smile as Megan found her in the kitchen.

"I'm so sorry, Beth, I fell back to sleep after Gregory left. I'm just no' feeling too well lately."

Beth narrowed her eyes. "Is yer stomach still giving ye trouble?"

"Aye. I think I ate something along the road on the way back that my stomach dinna care for."

"Have ye seen Emma?"

"Nay. I thought it would just go away, but I think 'tis time to see if she has something I can take to make me feel better."

Beth grinned and rubbed her swollen stomach. She gave Megan a slight shove on the shoulder. "Go see our healer."

Megan took the short walk to the healer's room and was greeted by shouting.

"Ye doona ken what ye're doing or I would be fixed by now and back in battle." It was obviously the grumpy patient.

She opened the door to see Emma bent over the warrior who had been brought in during the Gunn and Sinclair skirmish.

The healer sighed. "Ye are an *ejiit*, Gunn. How many times do I have to tell ye the battle's been over for weeks."

He growled. "The Gunns are always in a battle."

She shook her head. "And I have also told ye many times that I'm not sure ye will regain the use of yer legs. 'Twill take time."

The glower on the warrior's face had her stepping back, but she shook her head at Emma. The woman had the most patience of anyone she'd ever known.

Emma placed her hands on her hips and took several deep breaths. "If ye keep this up, Morgan Gunn, I will place ye in the dungeon."

The man narrowed his eyes. "Ye wouldn't do that. The laird would no' allow that since I am no' a prisoner. And I would kill anyone who tries to do that."

"With what? Ye canno' walk and ye have no sword. Do ye

think ye can chase me around the room to get a weapon?"

Morgan Gunn reached out and pulled Emma close, but Megan heard him say, "If I chase ye around the room, lass, it won't be to get a weapon." He released her and smirked.

The healer turned from the bed and her eyes grew wide when she saw Megan standing there. "'Tis sorry I am ye had to hear that." She shook her head and linked her arm with Megan's. "Let's take a walk in the garden and ye can tell me what ye came for and I can regain my self-control."

As they stepped into the garden, Emma took a deep breath.

"Are ye well, Emma?"

She smiled. "Aye. I just need to get away from my patient every once in a while." She looked at Megan. "'Tis the mon who came in during that short battle when ye were taken. He is improving, but I canno' tell if he will completely heal and walk again."

She stopped to look around the garden. "I doona like when the summer ends and all the beautiful flowers die."

She was quiet with her thoughts for a minute, then turned to Megan. "I am so sorry, I dinna even ask ye why ye came to see me. Are ye having a problem?"

Megan nodded as they sat on a large tree branch that was used as a bench. "Aye. I've been feeling sick since Gregory and I returned from Edinburgh."

Emma's brows rose. "That long? Why dinna ye come to see me before now?"

Megan shrugged. "I've been busy and kept thinking whatever food I ate that started this would eventually leave me."

"Tell me what yer suffering from."

"My stomach has been troubling me. I even bring up my dinner from the night before each morning."

Emma nodded. "Go on."

"I am so weary and weepy that I think Gregory is going to find a different bedchamber for himself."

By now, Emma was grinning. "When was the last time ye

had yer women's courses?"

Megan frowned. "I doona ken. I'm sure it was before I was taken by the men and brought to Edinburgh. Maybe a week or so before that."

"Megan, I am sure ye are pregnant."

Megan stared at her, a blank expression on her face. After almost a full minute, her eyes filled with tears. "Nay, Emma. I am barren."

"Who told ye that?"

"One of the maids at Sinclair Castle Girnigoe." She wiped the tears that had fallen on her cheeks. She started to laugh. "Do ye see what I mean, Emma? I'm weepy all the time."

Emma tapped her chin with her finger. "What made her tell ye that?"

Megan cleared her throat and looked away, sure she couldn't say this in front of Emma after having gone through it with the maid. "I asked Maggie who seemed to enjoy the attentions of men what my problem was with the marriage bed." Her face grew so hot she thought she would explode.

"I assume ye doona mean the mattress was uncomfortable."

"Nay." Megan took a deep breath. "After a year of marriage, I decided to finally ask someone who I was certain kenned a lot about it."

"Which was...?"

"Robert had a hard time entering me." She knew her face must be as red as a Fall apple, and she waved her hand in front of her face.

Emma reached out and took Megan's hand. "Was it painful for ye?"

"Aye! If 'twas no' my duty as a wife to allow my husband to do that, I would have moved to a different bedchamber, or even to my own bothy in the village."

Emma gave her a small smile. "So where does the being barren come in?"

"She said the reason I was having a problem was because I

must be barren."

Emma shook her head in confusion. "There is no connection that I am aware of between difficulty in the marriage bed and the lack of ability to conceive a babe."

Megan turned on the tree stump so she faced Emma. "But the whole time Robert and I were married, I ne'er became with child."

"First of all, if there is no child in the marriage, 'tis no' always the woman's fault. Sometimes a man's seed is no' strong enough." Before Megan could comment, Emma added. "Can I ask ye a personal question?"

Megan took in a deep breath. "Aye. I've already told ye more than I had even told the maid."

"Do ye have the same problem with Gregory?"

"Nay!" She shook her head. "Not at all."

"There is no problem with him entering ye?"

She grinned. "Nay, in most cases he slides right in." She began to fan her face with her hand again and gulped. "I canno' believe I just said that."

Emma took her by the hand and drew her up, once more linking their arms. "What yer friend the maid told ye was wrong. Some women's bodies take a little bit longer to be ready for their husbands. There is nothing wrong with that, just the way she is.

"However, if the man is anxious and thinking only of his pleasure, he might no' take the time to prepare his wife. And then it could be painful, which would make the wife tense up every time, making it worse."

Megan said nothing for a few minutes as they strolled, enjoying the lovely Fall day. Then she turned to Emma. "I'm with child."

Emma laughed. "Aye, I am sure ye are. I will want to see ye every couple of weeks. But in the meantime, eat a lot of healthy food—this stomach issue will clear up soon—get plenty of rest, and take long walks in the garden."

✥

GREGORY DUMPED A bucket of water over his head and dried his hair with one of the linens the maids left next to the water for the warriors to use when they were finished training.

He was anxious to get back to the keep and see Megan. He was a little concerned about how she'd been feeling lately. Hopefully, she hadn't picked up some illness from all the bad air and garbage in Edinburgh.

He found her sitting on their bed, just staring into space. He dropped his sword and other implements and joined her. "What did Emma say, my love?"

She looked at him with wonder in her eyes. "I am with child."

"I thought…"

Megan nodded. "I thought so too, but before we speak more about it, I want ye to hold me in yer arms while I cry again."

And he did.

And she did.

THE END

I hope you enjoyed Megan and Gregory's story. Please leave a review at Amazon where you can find more of my books.

Would you like to know how the battles between Emma Mackenzie and Morgan Gunn progress? Watch for *A Highlander's Heart*, book number three, coming in June, 2026.

About the Author

USA Today bestselling author, Callie Hutton, has penned more than sixty-eight historical romance books and Victorian Cozy Mysteries with humor and "historic elements and sensory details." (The Romance Reviews). Ms. Hutton's cozy mystery book, The Sign of Death was a finalist in the Simon and Schuster Mary Higgins Clark award in 2022. With close to a million novels sold and translated into several languages, she continues to entrance readers with her heartfelt stories.

www.calliehutton.com
facebook.com/calliehuttonsbooks
instagram.com/p/DEfvx2vOJ4S